THE BLACK CITY

THE BLACK CITY

GEORGE SAND

Translated by Tina A. Kover

Carroll & Graf Publishers
New York

THE BLACK CITY

Carroll & Graf Publishers
An Imprint of Avalon Publishing Group Inc.
245 West 17th Street
New York, NY 10011

First Carroll & Graf edition 2004

Originally published in France in 1860.

Library of Congress Cataloging-in-Publication Data is available.

ISBN: 0-7867-1324-0

Printed in the United States of America
Interior design by Paul Paddock
Distributed by Publishers Group West

THE BLACK CITY

CHAPTER I

Why so sad, my friend? What could be bothering you? You're young and strong, without any family to tie you down. You're a good worker, and your services are always in demand. No one thinks less of you because you were not born in these parts; in fact, everyone respects your conduct and your talents, especially because you're so well educated for a laborer. You can read and write and figure as well as any clerk. You have spirit; you have a good, logical head on your shoulders. And, on top of all that, you are the best-looking young man in town. Only twenty-four years old! I don't understand why you keep to yourself so much, instead of spending Sundays with us. You act as if you were better than everyone else, like we're not worthy of your company!"

The speaker was Louis Gaucher, knife maker, and he addressed his words to Etienne Lavoute, nicknamed Sept-Epées—Seven Blades—for his skill as a metalsmith. They sat in the sun in front of one of the five or six factories crowded on the banks of the river in this place called Trou-d'Enfer, Hell-hole. When conversing so close to the violent, magnificent waterfall, they had learned to snatch their words from the tangle of noise created by the turbulent water as well as hammers, the shrieking of metal tools, and the wheezing of the great furnaces.

The two men ate while they talked; in his lap Gaucher balanced a bowl of soup that had been delivered with proud gravity by his eldest daughter, aged five. His wife had followed with their younger child to keep watch over the little girl, and now the children romped together on the sandy riverbank while the woman, seeing her husband in the midst of conversation, remained several discreet paces away, though she occasionally glanced to make sure he was enjoying his meal.

Sept-Epées ate like a young boy, with his hands, and with the indifference common to those who have neither wife nor mother. Like his friend's, his arms were bare and covered with black stains, and the midday sun beat down on his uncovered head. The weather outside was cool, though, compared to the devilish heat of the forge.

Sept-Epées did not answer his friend. He acknowledged the concern with a handshake, then lowered his head and stared at the rushing water.

"Come on," Gaucher persisted, "something is troubling you. Is it anything I can help you with? Say something! I'm your friend—I want to help you."

"Thank you," the young man replied with a hint of pride in his voice. "I know you have a good heart, and if I needed anything from you I would ask, but truly, I do not—and as for money, you know as well as I that I could earn twelve francs a day if I requested it."

"Then why haven't you requested it? Are you so afraid of hard work?"

"No, but even if I doubled my daily earnings, would that truly be such an advancement?"

"Of course! You would be able to take longer rest periods, and you could stop working while you were still young. If I did not have a family to feed—and if I had your talent, of course—I should like to start my own factory in ten years or so."

"Yes, yes—you would become an overseer, pay and supervise the workers, keep the books, conduct business, all to buy a piece of land in the Upper Town in ten years and build an enormous house that will only bankrupt you? I call that the madness of wealth, which is what the workers aspire to around here."

"And why not?" returned Gaucher. "Any factory worker can become a comfortable middle-class citizen if he has a little intelligence. Look there, right above our heads, on the mountainside—pretty little streets and stairways, open lanes where a man can see fifty leagues to the horizon, pink and white walls with trellises and green vines climbing them, flowering gardens—and all of it sprang from this abyss we toil in from morning to night with our wheels and tongs, our hammers and iron bars. All those people who look down from their comfortable height and watch us sweat, while they read their newspapers and trim their rose bushes, are friends or children of the old laborers who worked all their lives to give them what they now have. They don't think less of us because we wear leather aprons. We can feel envy for them, but never hatred, because they expect us—or at least some of us—to rise just as they have risen. Look—it's not so very far! Two or three hundred meters of rock separate the hell we live in and that paradise beckoning us, rock that represents twenty years of courage and fortitude—it is all there; I dreamed of it all, too. But love found me, and then the children came. Men who marry young lose their chance for professional success, to be sure, but they have their wives and children to console them. That is why, even though I am bound to follow the same routine for the rest of my life, I never complain—I simply take each day as it comes."

"There is your proof," said Sept-Epées, "that there are only two choices in life: to be poor and happy, or to pursue wealth and gain misery along with it. I find myself caught between these two ideas, and I do not know which to choose. That is why I am—not sad, as you think, but worried, and I change my life's goal every day without finding one that satisfies me."

"I see that you are one of those men who has too many irons in the fire—one of them is bound to burn. You always dwell on the negative side of things, and so you live in a hell of your own making. What is the spirit for, if not to seize upon the good things in life? I am not a great businessman, and I do not seek to become one. I look around me, and, because I decided to marry the girl I loved, I am content to remain in the Lower Town forever. Farewell, painted house with your shutters open to the breeze! Farewell, stone fountains flowing with cool water! Farewell to the young laborer's dream!

"Bah! Our 'hell' is not so miserable as they say. My eyes

have grown used to it, with its smoke-blackened roofs and trembling footbridges spanning the water, where I hear the clicking of carriage wheels and all the other noises that ring in the ears yet do nothing to prevent the craftsman from dreaming; and where I see children dirty with sweat and dust, children who turn pink again on Sunday and flutter like butterflies among the rocks, after trailing all week like ants about the machines—yes, all of it dances before my eyes and sings in my ears! I love the crude music of work, and if by chance I have a sad thought, I have only to get out a little, to come here and watch the water flowing and the sun shining, to feel proud and content. Yes, proud! After all, we live in a place that the devil would never really choose to inhabit, and we have made it our own world. We have tamed a mountain; we have harnessed a wild river and made it work for us more efficiently than thirty thousand horses could; we have built our homes on the very cliffs that our children dare not approach too closely, near the very waterfalls whose roar lulls them to sleep more gently than a mother's lullaby.

"You must remember, for three hundred years now, we have worked this narrow valley and made our families comfortable here. We began, little by little, at our own peril, struggling against nature, against the perils of commerce, which can be even more stubborn and menacing than nature itself. And now, in this black crevasse of rock, in this maze of waterfalls we call the Lower Town, we are now eight thousand pairs of hands strong, eight thousand men who can live their lives from birth to death without too much worry. Up there, instead of a lowly settlement, a rich town grew, a town built in soft colors that travelers compare to an Italian village, a new town with fountains, buildings, streets! That is something, my friend, to live in a place where men are neither slothful nor lazy, and where the people of the Upper Town may look with pride at the smoke plumes of the Lower Town, rising into the air like smoke from incense lit in honor of those who allowed them to grow and prosper!"

"You are right," replied Sept-Epées, "and your courage does much to lift my spirits! Yes, it is lovely, our Lower Town, our Black City, as it is known in these parts. I remember my astonishment when I arrived here to complete my apprenticeship. I was only twelve years old, I had always lived in the country, about twenty-five leagues from here, and I had just lost my mother and father. My heart was still bruised. I had no one left in the world except for my godfather, who returned to the region to care for me. He had left the region some time before, but came back so he could teach me what he considered a suitable trade, namely, his own. I was quite desolate; my parents had left me nothing, and I barely remembered my godfather and so had difficulty accepting the idea of obeying him. If the mayor and the curate of my village had not spoken sternly to me, I would have stayed at home. As it was, I could do nothing except cry as I traveled along the road that led me out of town, and when I came to the Black City, I was overcome by fear. I climbed to the Upper Town; I was quite intimidated and dared to speak to no one. When I asked where the Lower Town was, people laughed in my face.

'If you're looking for the Lower Town, my boy, you should

not have climbed one step. You must go down again, and there is a narrow passageway that will take you straight there.' So down I went, past the gardens, along the cliffs and finally into the little streets where men must walk single-file, and I dared to ask after my godfather, Father Laguerre. I was told: 'Go down still further, to Trou-d'Enfer, and you will see on your left the shop where he works.'

"I thought they were making fun of me. Trou-d'Enfer, indeed—Hellhole! I came from the flat country, and I knew nothing of cliffs. And to think of a hellhole in the midst of a town—it seemed impossible. And then I heard the roar of the waterfall. By then, night had fallen, and by the light from hundreds of furnaces I saw the waterfall lit up in red, and it did seem to me that I was gazing upon the rush and flow of fire. I was near my salvation! And so I gathered up my courage and stepped onto a footbridge. Near the middle of it, I believed I felt the brush of flames, and I thought myself lost. But finally I arrived here, just where we are sitting now, and I turned to look at the abyss. My head spun; I became dizzy, but my astonishment and delight at finding myself in this new place soon overcame my discomfort. I felt myself so far from my home that it seemed impossible ever to return there, and I said to myself, 'So—I'll spend the rest of my days at the bottom of Hell! Fancy that!'

"The next day, my godfather took me round the factories and workshops, to show me the town and help me orient myself. I had thought at first that all the factories were joined to make one enormous whole, but I soon discovered that they were as different from each other as are the many currents in the river. I noticed great numbers of men and children, black with soot, coming and going among the warehouses and footbridges. 'They are the gunsmiths, the cutlers, the locksmiths,' my godfather told me, 'the men of fire. And look, over there, at those other men, so clean and white, with hands as soft as a woman's. They are the paper-makers—the men of water. Look closely, my son, because you have never yet seen a sight to equal this one. There is nothing in the world more beautiful than the sight of these men working, so alive, so strong, each so dedicated to his own task: those men there can coax a mixture from the clay, which they stretch and smooth as if it were the finest cloth, and those men there can forge a bar of metal, and work it so skillfully that in less than twenty minutes you will see it transformed into a sturdy and capable tool!'

"I thought I must be dreaming. I spent the whole of that day watching those men working as joyfully as if they were at play, treating the resistant materials of their trades like the most malleable stuff in the world. I thought the paper even more astonishing than the metal, but iron seemed to me more masculine, and I was content to allow my godfather to steer me in that direction.

"After that first Sunday morning, he set me to work. You know well what kind of man Father Laguerre is; how he continues to battle iron and fire despite his seventy-two years. He bade me watch him, and when I was distracted—quite a natural occurrence at my age—he shouted so that I trembled, and threatened me with his hammer as if he meant to crack my skull.

"My fear of him did not last long. I soon saw that he was the very best man I had ever met, and in spite of his pretense of irritation he was as protective of me as a true parent. I was never tempted to abuse his largesse—boredom incited me to work. I envied the children younger than myself who were already useful and skilled in a craft. I was afraid they would jeer at me—but ambition overtook shame, and, as you can see, I learned my trade as quickly as those who had begun long before me.

"And now, you see, I have been working here for twelve years! For nearly four of them, I have earned as much as the most skilled craftsman, and I've been able to put aside a little money. No one finds fault with me; our employers trust me implicitly, and I should be well pleased with my situation. I know—I feel—that work is a noble thing, and I have no reason to be unhappy. If I am, I'm well aware that it's my own fault."

Gaucher wanted to question his friend about this last reflection, for he sensed in him the impatience of a truly frustrated soul, but at that moment the factory bell sounded the end of the noon meal. Gaucher, being a dutiful worker, gave the soup bowl to his wife, kissed his children, and returned to work. He resolved to press Sept-Epées on the point he had raised as soon as time and leisure permitted it.

Sept-Epées, however, remained sitting on the riverbank, lost in thought. Finally, rousing himself to follow the example of his friend, he was turning back toward the factory when he saw Gaucher's wife approaching.

"Sept-Epées," she said, "have you told my husband what is bothering you?"

"No, Lise," he replied, "we were talking of other things."

"Then you made a mistake," said Lise, "for my Louis gives very good advice, and I thought he might help you to resolve things. You know you cannot go forever without giving Tonine a definite answer. That is not the way honest men behave."

Sept-Epées shrugged—not in a dismissive fashion, but to indicate that he was painfully aware that he could not give Lise the answer she wished.

He seemed so downcast that Lise took pity on him. "Come and have supper with us tonight," she said. "Perhaps then you'll feel better able to confide in Louis."

"You haven't told him anything!"

"Indeed I haven't, because you promised me you would do so yourself."

"Give me twenty-four hours more," said Sept-Epées, "or I will not come to supper tonight. No, wait—yes—I will come; I'll try to come." And he returned to work, leaving young Madame Gaucher less than satisfied with his answer, and quite worried about the future, for Tonine's sake.

CHAPTER II

Tonine Gaucher was a first cousin of Louis Gaucher. An orphan like Sept-Epées, she had nothing in the world except her two capable hands. She worked as a folder in the paper factory, just across from the cutlery works that employed both her cousin and her lover.

Indeed, Sept-Epées was besotted with Tonine, and he had implied his desire to court her when he asked her to walk with him on Sundays; but she had refused this request, saying, "Ask my cousin's permission, and his wife's, for they are the only family I have, and I cannot make a decision without their advice."

"You don't wish to speak to them about me yourself?" Sept-Epées had asked.

"No—it isn't my responsibility to do so. If I were to mention you, they would think that I had my heart set upon you, and I'm not certain of that yet."

This answer, containing more pride than tenderness, had taught Sept-Epées that he must be nothing but honest and direct with Tonine.

Tonine was only eighteen years old, but she had already

experienced enough of life to give her cause for reflection. She had witnessed a drama in her own family that had much bruised and battered her young heart. Her older sister, Suzanne Gaucher, had been the most beautiful girl in the region, and had taken a fancy to a stranger. He had once been a factory worker and was now owner of the largest factory in the Lower Town, where, thanks to a number of lucky investments, he had made a fortune. Suzanne had been clever and ambitious—she knew he was the man she must marry.

Upon becoming Mrs. Molino, she had taken her orphaned younger sister into her household, less from affection than out of distaste for the usual duties of the factory wife—thus, at fourteen years of age, Tonine already did the work of two. Suzanne had intended to have her sister properly educated and raised to be a well-bred young lady, but such dreams were short-lived. Molino, like most passionate men, was fickle of temperament. Within months, he had grown tired of his wife. He mistreated her, neglected her, and cheated on her. She died of shame before the year was out, while giving birth to a stillborn child.

Molino was grief-stricken and repentant at first, but he soon sought solace in his former vices, and became a pariah in the Black City. Even gentle Louis Gaucher regarded him with disgust. He eventually closed his factory and moved to the Upper Town, leaving Tonine to fend for herself with the excuse that she was an insolent child who refused to have anything to do with him.

In truth, Tonine would have preferred death to her

brother-in-law's charity. She had watched his behavior with horror, and she understood all too well Suzanne's heartbreak and despair. At fifteen, after a year's absence from work, she returned to the paper factory as poor as she had been when she left, but pragmatic and newly courageous as well.

Others in her place might have been jeered at or mocked for a family misadventure of which so many had initially been envious, but if Suzanne had assumed an air of grandeur with her old friends, no one could reproach Tonine for similar behavior. She had lived shabbily in spite of her sister's wealth, and her home life with the Molinos had brought her nothing but embarrassment and pain.

Tonine was not as beautiful as her sister had been at eighteen. She was tall, slender and pale. She bore herself with a sort of elegant gravity that distinguished her from other young women her age. Her eyes and voice were gentle and soft, and some thought she might even surpass Suzanne in loveliness one day.

Tonine also possessed a remarkable elegance of manner that could not be attributed to her brief association with wealth—Molino had been badly brought up, and wealth had not induced him to keep a better sort of company. Neither Suzanne nor Tonine had often had the opportunity to enjoy quality companionship. Suzanne, vain and shallow, had remained rather common, whereas Tonine's pride, wisdom, and grace had only grown more marked. Possessed of inherent good taste, she admitted that, however much she had resented her brother-in-law's handouts, she had enjoyed pampering herself and, during her frequent walks in the

Upper Town, she still displayed a sense of innate dignity. She cut down and altered her shabby dresses to make them even more stylish than those of the other girls, and carefully protected her clothes from the slightest hole or stain.

Tonine avoided dances, even after the mourning period for her sister had ended. She refused to join in her friends' raucous games, and she never allowed young men to ruffle her composure—to look at her, one would think she belonged to a different world than that of her contemporaries. She had a talent for making herself liked; everyone around Tonine tried to please her, and some girls even attempted to imitate her distinctive style.

Sept-Epées was the only young man who had ever dared to court Tonine, and he soon regretted his decision. He had done it partly for the challenge, as a test—at first, at least—of his own self-esteem, but he soon grew to care for her deeply. When he received scant encouragement, he admonished himself not to care, but to no avail. The day Lise invited him to supper, he tried to explain himself to his godfather.

Father Laguerre, observing that Sept-Epées seemed listless and distracted, had asked in his gruff, fatherly way if the young man was really as smitten with Tonine as he appeared to be. "Yes—I care for her more than I ever intended to," admitted the youth. "I believe that she has cast some sort of spell over me. Ever since I met her, when I was still a crude peasant and she already so much more refined than I was, in spite of her being younger, I've watched her. It always seemed to me that she knew I was different from the other boys, just as I knew she was different from the other girls. I sensed that she possessed a dignity that other girls did not. I saw how she kept to her studies, how she never encouraged the boys to approach her. I always thought her the most beautiful of the young girls—she is the most elegant, the most fastidious and graceful, and you yourself have nicknamed her 'princess.' I wanted to make her happy, and I thought she knew this, and appreciated me for it. I believed she would accept my courtship.

"But when I approached her, she immediately sent me to speak to her relatives. I believed we should get to know each other before becoming engaged, and I was upset by her presumption. I didn't speak to her for a month. I thought she would be shocked by my actions, and that she would approach me, even if it was to reprove me—but she seemed to forget me instantly; she was just as calm, as indifferent, as always. I concluded that she thought I was not worthy of her, but at last I did speak to her again. Then, for the first time, I saw her laugh—and it was at me that she laughed. 'I believe my cousin and his wife must not approve of you at all,' she said, 'for they haven't yet mentioned your suit to me.'

"Then I felt ashamed for having said nothing to her family, and I decided to confide my feelings to Lise—but casually, in conversation, so as not to entangle myself too deeply. Lise was pleased by this, and said she would speak to her husband.

"I told Lise I didn't want to compromise my relationship with Louis, who is not only my friend but Tonine's guardian and, for all intents and purposes, her brother, unless I was sure that Tonine cared for me, at least a little. Lise thought this reasonable and promised to let me go to Gaucher first. As to Tonine's feelings for me, Lise either could not or would not tell me anything. Perhaps she didn't want to reveal too much until she knew that I was firmly set upon marriage.

"This has been my situation for the past three months—nothing changes. When I visit Tonine in spite of my reservations, she seems indifferent—even cool. Lise invariably tries to persuade me to speak with her husband, and you know very well that the moment I do so, I will be irreversibly betrothed. This would suit me quite well if I knew for certain that Tonine loved me, but since I still have doubts on that score, I must wait until she tells me so herself. It's a serious thing to get married—I want to know for certain that my wife cares for me!"

"Ah," nodded Laguerre, "now I understand. Would you like me to explain to the princess that you will stop this silly hesitation the moment you know for certain that she wants you?"

Sept-Epées did not answer. "Well?" prodded the old man with growing irritation. "So you want the girl but not the marriage, is that it? I must say, you are behaving quite stupidly! The Upper Town is full of women of low character, and yet you act so foolishly with Tonine, an honest working girl!"

Sept-Epées was accustomed to hearing his godfather disparage the Upper Town. In contrast to Gaucher, who took pride in its accomplishments, Laguerre harbored a curmudgeonly dislike of the neighboring village and enjoyed boasting that he had willingly set foot there only three times in his life. A tireless worker with a loyal heart and a narrow mind, the old man had no patience for upstarts. He resented the comfortable lifestyles of those in the Upper Town and, from his vantage point in the Black City, condemned even the simplest of pleasures as unholy vices, as anathemas to the dignity of the workers among whom he lived.

Laguerre's straitlaced attitude was of great civic benefit to the Black City. He had no acquaintance outside his parish, but within the borders of his chosen world he was a hero, a model of stoic pride and uncompromising faith. No Roman senator was ever prouder of his position in life, and no king ever displayed such paternal pride in his realm.

Sept-Epées laughed to himself at his godfather's zeal and refused to argue with him. He swore to Laguerre that he had never wanted to seduce any girl from the Black City, least of all Tonine—and if this last statement was not completely true, it was perhaps because the young man was not yet completely aware of the depth of his own feelings.

A little calmer, Laguerre nevertheless continued to admonish his godson. "What are the young people about these days? Nothing makes you happy, and it seems to me that the entire world has gone crazy. Even a strong and honest young woman cannot please you if she doesn't flirt and chase after you herself! Look at you, besotted, yet demanding that the woman you love beg you to marry her! Stop it, will you? You're acting like a fool, and if I were Tonine I would tell you to go fawn on another doorstep and stay clear of mine!"

Sept-Epées shook his head in frustration. "No. Tonine leaves me hope, because she hasn't told me that I have waited too long, or that she doesn't wish to speak to me again. Today, Lise pressed me for a decision and hinted that Tonine may have received another proposal. That is why I have come for your advice, godfather—I implore you, try to give it without getting too angry."

"I can't imagine why you're asking me," the old man replied in a softer tone. "You seem to be telling me that you fear marrying too early. In my opinion, you are wrong—people should marry young, so that they have time to raise children. But it may be that Tonine is not interested in you, or that you haven't yet given marriage enough thought. If that is the case, the truthful path is the best one. You should break with this girl and tell Lise so right away, so that she can give Tonine the news; then, after a little time has passed, you can begin to pursue someone else. The most important thing is that you do not insult the cousin of your good friend Gaucher, and you can give no offense if you are honest and apologize for behavior that may have been a little careless on your part. And that is all I have to say about it. Now look—it's eight o'clock. You must be up at dawn tomorrow. You'd better hurry if you want to speak to Lise. Be sure to put out the lamp when you come home, and don't forget to say your prayers."

This last admonition had been a daily ritual of Laguerre's during the entire twelve years that his godson had lived with him. He knew the boy was too sensible to set their house on fire and that, as for the prayer, Sept-Epées would make a half-hearted attempt at best; still, Laguerre reminded him each day for the benefit of his own conscience.

Sept-Epées made his way toward the Gauchers' home, his thoughts filled with the question of what to do. It was not as easy a situation to resolve as he had let Laguerre believe. He had not lied—Tonine had not encouraged him in words, nor had she fallen into despair at his hesitation, but she had suffered, and despite her efforts to keep a brave face, there had been tears in her eyes when she smiled. The young smith was too perceptive not to know that he was the cause. He felt that he was loved, and he felt guilty as a result of it.

However, he was quite a handsome young man and already a bit spoiled by the admiring glances of young women. His employers and the clients at his workshop tended to spoil him as well, with their enthusiasm for his handiwork. He had become intelligent through study and industrious through ambition; and because he found himself financially comfortable, thanks to his godfather's longtime provision of food and lodging, when most young people his age had more debt than wealth, he had allowed prosperity to go to his head. When he had spoken disdainfully of wealth to Gaucher, it had really been to defend himself against the temptations and dreams that assaulted him constantly.

Everything that Gaucher had said of the new bourgeoisie in the Upper Town, and of the ease with which an intelligent man could attain a share in that charmed life, burned in Sept-Epées's brain like a flame. His heart had made a hopeful leap as he—who trembled with ambition and feigned his prayers—listened to this wise friend who, without ambition of his own, opened the door to the future and nudged him over the threshold.

The conversation with Gaucher had so moved him that Lise's reproach and Laguerre's questions about Tonine had served only to push him farther away from the idea of marriage, especially a marriage where the bride could offer him no dowry but her virtue and grace.

He felt a bit better when he repeated Laguerre's words to himself: "Apologize frankly for your carelessness, and leave quickly so as not to aggravate your offenses." At the same time, he felt that the mistakes he had made were too serious not to warrant some guilt, and guilt does not often breed honesty.

He quickened his steps, hoping that Lise had not yet spoken to her husband and that Tonine was prudent enough not to prejudice Gaucher toward him with her complaints. Gaucher, in spite of his perpetual good humor, did not place reason above the honor of his family. He had been quite ready to pummel Molino. Sept-Epées, unlike Molino, was not a reprehensible man, and he loved Gaucher, and cherished his regard as well as Tonine's. He had no wish to make two sacrifices to his ambition rather than one.

When he approached his friend's house, he was trembling with fear and daring, with shame and hope, with resolution and uncertainty all mingled inside himself, and dividing him against himself.

Night had fallen. As he arrived at the Gaucher home, Sept-Epées saw two people, a man and a woman, sitting on a bench near the doorway. He recognized Gaucher's voice.

The woman, who had a child in her lap, seemed at first to be Lise, but upon closer examination he realized with shock that it was Tonine. She did not live with her cousin; she must have come to hear what had passed during the promised discussion—mentioned to her, no doubt, by Lise, who, he surmised, was in the house, putting her youngest child to bed.

CHAPTER III

Sept-Epées was thankful for the darkness, which hid the embarrassment he knew must be written on his face. He was usually able to maintain his composure when he felt himself to be in the right, but now when he tried to speak naturally, he tried in vain. Gaucher did not seem to see him, but Tonine, who had noticed him right away, came quickly to his aid.

"I think, my friend," she said in the pleasant manner that rarely deserted her, even when her heart was aching, "that you are not here so late to speak to Gaucher of the weather. Something must be weighing on your mind. Let me go and put Rosette to bed, and when I return after your conversation with my cousin, perhaps you'll wish to speak to me as well."

Sept-Epées thought he detected a hint of encouragement in her words that seemed to promise an end to his uncertainty. However, going on the defensive, as was his wont whenever he felt that his freedom was being threatened, he spoke quickly to prevent Tonine from leaving, and sat down across from her on a chair so that he was blocking her entrance to the house. "If I thought," he said, "that you were not resolved to reject me, perhaps I would wish to speak about what you're hinting of, but, today as always, you seem to be making fun of me."

"What?" interjected Gaucher, astonished and baffled at the turn the conversation had so quickly taken. "What is this? I would very much like to know what the two of you are talking about!"

"Explain it to him," Tonine said to Sept-Epées, "and let me take the baby in to her mother."

"Give her to me," said Lise, appearing in the doorway. "The three of you need to discuss this together. That is why Sept-Epées came here tonight, I believe—and you as well, Tonine. There is no reason for either of you to hold back any longer."

She took the infant and disappeared into the house. Gaucher, puzzled, urged Sept-Epées to speak. Tonine waited for what he would say. Sept-Epées, looking in vain for an escape, remained silent.

Tonine felt two large tears slide down her cheeks. Perhaps if he had seen them, Sept-Epées would have softened—but he did not see them, and Tonine realized that she would have to suffer alone.

"Don't worry, my friend," she said brightly, her tone one that required all her courage and pride to sustain, "I'm not your enemy, and I hold no grudge against you. You're an honest man and a good worker, but I could hardly think of getting married at my age. I'm far too young, and besides, I can't imagine that we would suit each other."

Sept-Epées was so struck by Tonine's dignity that he felt disappointment rather than relief at finding himself thus freed. "Ah," he said, "I see that I didn't mistake your feelings for me, and that I was right not to press you to marry me. It seems to me that you could have spared me the trouble of coming here to be rejected. You might have told me on the day I first spoke to you that I could never make you happy."

"So, it is I who am at fault," Tonine responded with a note of reproach so subtle that her bitterness was undetectable. She turned to Gaucher. "Let me say a word in my own defense. Please don't mistake me for a coquette, my cousin, for you know that is not my way. The truth is that your friend Sept-Epées told me months ago that he had some idea of courting me."

"That was wrong of him," Gaucher said. "He should have spoken to me first."

"It's true," acknowledged Sept-Epées, "I *was* wrong. I was proud, and I didn't want Tonine's decision to be affected by her family's opinions. I wanted her to decide for herself. You know well how proud I am."

"Besides," Tonine put in, "he meant to speak to you as soon as I accepted him. It was I who prevented him by withholding my answer."

Gaucher looked from one to the other. "The two of you seem a bit confused. Your stories do not agree. Sept-Epées is complaining that he was deceived from the beginning, and Tonine says the opposite. Are you both wrong?"

"Perhaps," said Tonine, "but neither of us is too far off. Sept-Epées spoke to me seriously and I responded to him in kind, but perhaps we misunderstood each other. He thought, wrongly, that I had changed my mind, and he waited to hear from me. I thought he had forgotten me, and I didn't tell him what I was thinking."

"And now," put in Sept-Epées, still wavering between disappointment and relief, "I understand things perfectly, and I can forget any dreams I may still have harbored."

"Wait!" cried Gaucher, who was too straightforward by temperament to understand all that was happening. "I see that you're disappointed, my friend, and now I understand why you've been so down these last few months, and why this morning you said you were unhappy despite your having a job you enjoy and enough money to live comfortably. It's love that has been bothering you! You want to know why Tonine is refusing you! Her reasons cannot be good ones—you would be quite a prize for her, and I don't see why you are not pleasing to her, or what you could have done to make her feel the way she does."

"So," said Tonine, laughing in spite of herself, "you are trying to make us argue? You believe that if I express my poor opinion of him, he will become angry and say disagreeable things to me?"

Sept-Epées dreaded an explanation that would somehow reinstate his relationship with Tonine, and even though he did not want to subject himself to criticism without defending himself, he urged her to tell her side of the story.

"Because you want me to speak as well," she said, "I will not hide anything from you. My opinion is this—you're too free-spirited to take on the responsibility of wealth. In my eyes, these ambitious qualities of yours are faults. When you spoke to me of marriage, Sept-Epées, you thought you were enticing me when you said you aimed to make a fortune. For every tool you make, you want to sell two, and you have ideas in your head for inventions that will make you the equal of any master. . . ."

"I was dreaming aloud," said Sept-Epées, confused and stung, "and I told you those things in secret, Tonine. You should have either forgotten them or kept them to yourself."

"If it is a secret," replied Tonine, "I can keep it, don't worry. I give nothing away by speaking in front of Gaucher. I will tell no one, but whether you were serious or not, it gave me much to think about. You said you didn't want to stay in the Black City. You came here as a young apprentice and you wanted to leave as a property owner and master of your own fortune. You said you wished to have a painted house with a garden in the Upper Town someday, and that your wife would wear silk gowns and your children would receive the best schooling."

"And what if he did say that?" Gaucher cried with his habitual naive enthusiasm. "Some have failed to attain this dream, it's true, but not everyone is as capable and resourceful as our Sept-Epées. Do you think, then, that he is consumed by ambition, and that he's putting the cart before the horse?"

"Yes," said Sept-Epées, feeling more and more wounded. "That is what she believes. She thinks I have a head full of empty dreams."

"You are wrong," responded Tonine. "I don't believe that.

In fact, I'm almost positive that you *will* be successful, because—" Here she broke off, pursing her lips.

"Because why?" interjected Gaucher, seeing that Tonine was about to keep her thought to herself.

"Because he is brave and capable," Tonine finished with a smile, while inside her head she cried, 'Because he will never love anyone!' "I, on the other hand," she continued, "have no intention of changing my station in life. You know all too well why I have reason to be fearful, after what I saw happen to someone very close to me! It's not that I think it impossible for a wealthy person to lead an honorable life, but I do believe that it would be very difficult for a middle-class man to remain content with a factory worker's daughter. We are simple creatures; we do not know how to be fashionable. The upper-class women mock us. I, too, am proud—it's perhaps my greatest flaw. I want to marry a man who is my equal, and someone whose eyes are fixed on the Upper Town could never be my husband. That is all I have to say—you see, Sept-Epées, I don't mean to offend you. Each man must follow his own happiness. Please, don't trouble yourself about me any longer. I hope you'll be able to put me out of your mind."

With that, Tonine withdrew. Lise, who had returned and was seated on the doorstep, ached to follow her, because she believed that at the bottom of her heart her cousin did love the handsome young smith—but it was useless. Tonine saw plainly that Sept-Epées's inclination to hold on to her was not strong enough.

"Well!" said Gaucher when Tonine had left. "She's quite

a girl, and I had not realized just how contemplative she is. She was scarred by what she saw happen to her poor sister, but her reasoning *is* faulty where you are concerned, and it's just as well for you that she will not marry you, my friend. A woman who thinks as she does is not for you. She would hold you back from your future success."

Sept-Epées gazed dreamily into the distance. "Do you really think I am destined for success?" he mused. "Be careful—if you don't, then you mustn't encourage me."

"My dear friend," responded Gaucher, "I cannot imagine what grand ideas you might have, and since I am no great scholar I'd be a poor judge of your inventions, but I told you something this morning and I'll say it again. If you earn twelve francs a day, you can save several thousand in just a few years, and you can open your own workshop. After that, you may be more or less successful—but whatever the case, there is nothing wrong with success, and I would be the last person to tell you there is. Men have the right to seek happiness, and it is perhaps even the duty of those who have the ability to seek it. One man's happiness encourages another's, and if ambitious men didn't have the example of lazy ones, they might lose their motivation. So, follow your path without letting yourself be swayed, either by your godfather, who believes that all the inhabitants of the Upper Town are damned, or by Tonine, who had a painful childhood and sees Molino in everyone. You're young, and you must embrace your freedom. Don't worry about love or marriage. You don't have a day—or even an hour—to waste, if you wish to make your fortune."

After Sept-Epées had taken his leave of Gaucher and Lise, the latter reproved her husband for the advice he had given his young friend. "And you—are you ambitious too?" she queried.

"My ambition is to make you happy," Gaucher replied frankly.

"It's all very well for you to say that," returned Lise, "but perhaps you regret marrying me just the same!"

"No!" Gaucher declared in a firm and ringing voice. "I would never have had the patience to amass a fortune for myself alone—and besides, without you I would not be good for anything."

He kissed his wife on both cheeks. Sept-Epées, in the lane outside, was still near enough to hear the tender words and resounding kisses. His heart twisted inside him. "Don't worry about love or marriage," Gaucher had said. "Should I not worry about pleasure or happiness either?" Sept-Epées asked himself. "Then with what should I occupy myself? Work? My own obstinacy? The unhappiness of my childhood? Suddenly, all my ambition doesn't seem like such a good thing."

Instead of returning home, Sept-Epées turned down the road leading out of town and climbed up along the riverbank. The night was dark, and in the deep canyon the only illumination came from the glints of light reflected in the river. "I should be overjoyed," Sept-Epées said to himself, "that I am free from the threat of marriage! Tonine is a brave girl, after all, for having put things to Gaucher in such a way that he had nothing to reproach me for. He thinks she's the one who refused me, and if I'd been forced to tell the truth, we would be in a dire situation now! Yes, yes, Tonine does have spirit, and prudence, and a generous heart."

Thus engrossed in his thoughts of Tonine, Sept-Epées began to regret that he had not courted her without reservation and to reflect that he had rejected her because he'd muddled the matter with too much thought. Then, with the changeability of youth, he felt wounded by the disdain that he sensed lay at the foundation of Tonine's refusal. Suppose she had spoken her true thoughts! Had she, at that moment, made a comparison between him and her brother-in-law and judged him capable of similar behavior? There is evidence of her irrationality, he said to himself. No—it was not possible that she equated him with the arrogance and vulgarity of Molino. When had she ever seen him act in any unfavorable way? When had he ever shown himself capable of becoming such a man? Was that the inevitable outcome of his desire for wealth? Were all intelligent men eventually tempted by unworthy pursuits?

Having convinced himself of Tonine's unfairness toward him, Sept-Epées now turned his examination squarely upon his own conscience, as if Tonine were there beside him. He tried to look at himself objectively, penetratingly, and inside his head he protested, "No—no, my heart is pure, and my mind is clear. I don't dislike working, and bourgeois vanity isn't blinding me. My goals are higher than that. I'm not a man who is able to work like a machine for his entire lifetime—any spirit with even a little nobility can only have a natural horror of slavery. Factory duties can wear a man down, but in business there is movement of ideas, of emotions, of varied interests, of calculations—there is a sort of passion that broadens the horizons of one's life. Should I, like my godfather, spend sixty years wrestling with an iron bar, always in the same way, perpetually molding metal into the same shape? My godfather is old! When he was young, being a soldier was the only worthy occupation. Today things are different—industry is king, and the young can achieve anything!"

Conversing thus with the shadow of Tonine, Sept-Epées felt a sadness overtaking him. The wind moaned around him, and the water murmuring at his feet seemed almost to sob. He turned involuntarily to make sure that he was indeed alone, and when he saw that in fact he was he became sadder still. Deep inside him was a voice even more plaintive than the water's rush, and it cried mournfully, "You will be alone forever."

At the same time, the ambition that never left him spoke up with a voice of its own, reassuring him. "Bah!" said the invisible counselor, "Tonine is perhaps a little less silly than the other girls, but that's all! She didn't really want you—she didn't want to be loved seriously, and a working girl like her would be an embarrassment to a man with a future like yours. She is pretty enough, but her white hands and graceful airs don't make up for her narrow views and populist vanity, which is the worst sort. Besides, if you loved her enough to sacrifice all your ambition and settle for a meager existence, you would be a bit stupid, a bit ignorant even, like our brave Gaucher. Once hope has deserted a man, he settles easily into the daily grind, and in time he doesn't even regret what might have been. He neglects himself, morally and physically. Lise is doubtless a good woman, intelligent enough, and when Gaucher married her she was in the bloom of youth, but what has she become after years of marriage? The very shadow of her former self, forever toting two children, thin and often shabbily dressed, all of which may be the epitome of virtue in a lower-class family but surely will not excite a husband's interest—unless, like Lise's husband, he too has lost his elegance and his inclination to take care of himself. Is this what would become of Tonine after her marriage? Then would your love quickly die, this love for which you sacrificed everything!"

Lost in thought, Sept-Epées found himself in the midst of a mountainous terrain that proved difficult to navigate in the dark. He stopped and braced himself against a boulder of granite so as not to tumble down the slope. He had lost his way, he no longer knew exactly where he was.

CHAPTER IV

Sept-Epées recognized nothing about his surroundings except a bend in the waterfall below him that highlighted, against the whiteness of its foam, the sharp black angle of a factory roof. Scattered all along the river were small workshops that seemed less and less significant in the shadows of the towering walls of granite separating them from the town. Some of these workshops were balanced so precariously on the riverbank that their workers risked being swept away by the tumultuous torrent on stormy days, or by the frequent rockslides there.

Sept-Epées pondered the strength and weakness of man struggling thus against the forces of nature, fighting for this treasure of a waterfall that might at any moment destroy his hopes, his work, his life. Instead of being horrified by the idea, he focused on the fact that one of the ramshackle factories, whose bizarre situation he was contemplating at that very moment, had recently been put up for sale, probably at a very low price, because the man who had built it had run through his few assets and was even now being threatened with eviction. "There," thought the ambitious young man, "there is the only serious danger of the worker's life: it is not being washed away by a waterfall or replaced by a machine; anyone who risks everything to achieve even more cares as little for his own skin as the soldier dashing into battle. No, it is the fear of not being able to muzzle that ferocious beast called luck, of seeing it escape after the twentieth attempt to cage it. If anything would drive a man to faithlessness and insanity, then that is it!"

But anything can be turned into fuel to feed one's passion, and instead of pitying the poor industrialist and questioning his chosen path, Sept-Epées thought only of profiting from another's misfortune. "I'm sure," he told himself, "that this place wouldn't sell for more than a couple of years' worth of my salary; another year would pay for machinery and tools. I have four years' worth of savings, and I can be my own employer tomorrow, if I wish—the owner of quite a small enterprise, to be sure, on the lowest rung of the ladder, but even that is rare and honorable at twenty-four years old. It would not take me long to make my little business prosper, and I could sell it at double, maybe even triple the price I paid, which would allow me to buy a much bigger place, and little by little I would work myself into the core of industry here—in moving down along the riverbank, I could cause my fortunes to climb!"

The metaphor buoyed the spirits of the young smith. When one is faced with great dilemmas of conscience, such a phrase can often be soothing; a mere word game promising a triumphant resolution. Simple and enthusiastic people are often fatalistic. Young Sept-Epées imagined that destiny had guided him to this wild place so that he could grasp the instrument of his future wealth.

He gathered his thoughts. He knew well that this was one of the most treacherous and least-visited places in Val d'Enfer. There was probably a fairly easy road that climbed to the Upper Town as well as a small mule path that followed alongside the torrent and made its roundabout way to the Lower Town. It was perhaps half a league each way, either by the road or the path along the bottom of the ravine.

This particular factory was known as the Shack—hardly the most promising name—and the spot where it was located had earned the ominous nickname of Lost Hollow. The rush of the river was quite strong there, and the rock was of excellent quality for building if one so desired. The products manufactured at the Shack were of the humblest sort, mainly farming tools, but the profusion of neighboring farms and villages on the other side of the mountain assured one a steady clientele, if one took the trouble to visit the local markets and fairs. At just a small additional cost, nails could be easily manufactured there as well.

Sept-Epées felt that these basic products lay a bit beneath him; he could temper well the blade of a sword or a lance and could forge such noble weapons with taste and precision, but, after all, one could apply intelligence and talent to the production of simple things as well, to make them lighter and more accurate, to produce a better plow or put a sharper sickle into a farmer's hands. Even the most rudimentary tool could be perfected and thus could its owner be induced to acknowledge the skill of its manufacturer.

Sept-Epées dreamed of a free and active existence. He envisioned himself as the owner of two or three strong mules to bear his merchandise to the surrounding farmers, or, even better, a good little mountain horse to carry him and his wares to towns and villages further away, where, thanks to his honest manners, his clear and correct language, and his appealing face, he could build a large clientele among the retailers. He would get to see open country—he would breathe clean air in fertile fields after these twelve years that he'd been closed within the hellish black crevasse of Trou d'Enfer! He would meet new people; he would be appreciated. Within a few years, his education and intelligence would make him a man of importance, one able to serve the public and enjoy ever-growing credit. He saw himself as a man on the rise, with no end in sight, no desire unsatisfied; a man of action, his conscience clean—except for the distant, secret shame of Tonine. Aside from the inner guilt he bore regarding her, his hopes and wishes would be entirely pure.

The more he contemplated the ramshackle building in Lost Hollow, the more he came to own it in his mind. "This pitiable site, this inhospitable place where a workshop has the audacity to stand—here I will be sole master of my own domain! I'll have workers and I will treat them more humanely than I was ever treated by those who have exploited my talent until today. I shall be the king of this solitary place—I shall face and vanquish this cascade of water and laugh at its outraged roar. I will plant my stake here for two or three years at the most. I'll have a few books;

I'll study and travel and learn my part. And I will leave here far cleverer than those who boast of knowing everything without ever having read anything. Then, perhaps, Tonine will regret that she let me leave the Black City without telling me she was wrong, without trying to make me stay."

The Shack's owner was one Audebert, whom Sept-Epées knew only a little, but who seemed to be a man of slow wits. Sept-Epées had seen him occasionally but felt inclined to keep his distance. Audebert was something of a gossip, an idle talker, who presumed himself a gentleman and gained only the dismissive shrugs of serious-minded men. He had not been seen in the Black City for some time; he had been coming and going in the surrounding areas quite a bit lately, in an effort to settle his affairs, and he inspired confidence in no one. He was currently thought to be in Lyon. His creditors had threatened to seize all his possessions if he did not return with money at the beginning of next week, or so Sept-Epées had heard an acquaintance tell his godfather several days before.

Sept-Epées was startled when, as he prepared to regain the road back to town, he saw a shaft of light emanate from the abandoned factory and glint off the wet stones jutting out of the torrent.

"Ah," he thought to himself, "this is truly my destiny! If I were a superstitious man, I would be certain that some good or evil spirit had brought me here, either to my success or my ruin! I must go, now, on my very first exploration of this place."

Guided by the mysterious illumination, Sept-Epées made

his way down from rock to rock until he reached the factory's main door. It was closed; the shaft of light, he noted, gleamed from an opening in the upper gallery. No movement suggested the presence of any other human being.

Sept-Epées knocked; but whether the rush of the waterfall drowned his rap on the door or no one deigned to respond to it, he did so in vain. His curiosity increased by the silence, he observed that the shaft of light was directed toward a boulder right in the middle of the water just opposite the factory. The way the light was reflected off the water allowed Sept-Epées to see the interior of the building, and what he saw was quite strange.

A man, alone in the warehouse, had his back turned to the light, which glinted off the crown of his bald head. His brow, in profile, appeared to be high like that of an intellectual's, but its slope indicated a lack of depth to his thought. He was busily writing on the wall with a piece of charcoal. The handwriting was weak, sprawling. When he was finished, he turned fully around, and Sept-Epées recognized poor Audebert, his face pale, with burning eyes. He took up a rope, and with meticulous concentration fashioned a peculiar knot that he repeated several times, then he retreated into shadow.

A dark thought flashed through Sept-Epées's mind. He strained to make out what was written on the wall, and read the following poorly spelled words: "I dye by my own hand out of shayme and guilt at having lost everything. I have alwais been an honest man. Pray for my soul." Sept-Epées realized that he had just witnessed the preparations for a suicide, and with new urgency he was reaching for the door handle when the unfortunate man reappeared. Audebert approached the wall upon which he had written his parting statement; he erased the word *dye*, then wrote something else, only to erase it as well and rewrite the original choice. His uncertainty probably stemmed from the fact that his knowledge of spelling was quite limited, and he was anxious to be clearly understood by those who would read this last message—it was also possible that a last vestige of dignity preoccupied him at this, his final moment.

Sept-Epées frantically searched his mind for a way to dissuade Audebert from his morbid project. The door was locked, and it might be too late by the time he was finally able to break it down. An idea struck him, and he cried at the top of his lungs, "Hurry, my friends, over here! Help me!"

Audebert would not have been human if, at the very moment of ending his own life, he had not been distracted by the prospect of saving someone else's. The poor old man, whose neck was already in the noose, rushed outside and saw Sept-Epées coming toward him. Elated at the success of his strategy, the youth seized Audebert by the arms.

"You scared the devil out of me, you rascal," said poor Audebert when both parties had explained themselves, "but my chance is not lost."

"I think your plan is a terrible one, old man," the young smith said, entering the factory with Audebert. "I know you have neither wife nor children, but surely you have friends!"

"I have no more friends," Audebert returned wearily, "and when everything I own is sold, my debts still will not be settled."

"Well, then—honor dictates that you work until they are!"

"It does indeed—but my strength is gone, and I am good for nothing. I would rather die than be a beggar."

Sept-Epées thought the best way to distract the man might be to urge him to relate his troubles. He hastened to ask a few questions.

"My story is not a happy one," responded the old man. "I was married once, and a father, just like your godfather Laguerre, who knows me well and also knows that I have never wronged anyone. We were friends in our youth, and our relationship ended because I wouldn't follow his advice. After we both lost our wives and children to illness when we were forty years old or so, our paths diverged. Your godfather's idea was to save money for his old age—an idea that has not prevented him from reaching that old age without the slightest concession to comfort! A man who is in love with money can never have enough, and the less he spends, the more he wishes to have. I don't mean to say that your godfather is greedy; I know he is good to you, and I believe he'll leave you his fortune—and since I have heard that you are a good lad, his scrupulousness will not be wasted. As for me, I acted differently. Life dealt me an unfortunate hand, but I still believe I was right. Why else would I tell you my opinions! Surely, you must think like Laguerre."

"No," protested Sept-Epées. "I do not think like him; that is why I am by no means sure that he will leave anything to me. I hope to leave the Black City soon, and I know well that after that day he will have no interest in what becomes of me—but we're talking of you, and I assure you that you can tell me your views without fearing my censure."

"Ah, well, that is different! I see that you too crave action, but I do not know that you completely understand my way of thinking, and so I'll explain it to you—it will probably be the last time I tell anyone. God, I suppose, has sent me a fine young man who will bear witness to my good character after I am no longer here to defend myself. That candle there will soon flicker out, but I believe it will last longer than I! Let us go and sit on the riverbank. If I'm to remain in this world a little longer, let me at least see the stars tonight. There was not a single star in the sky when despair at last overtook me, and now it is a little lighter—a bit like my heart, which benefits from the sincerity of your own. But the dark nights will return, my son, and with them an idea blacker than a tomb—the idea that I am beloved by no one."

"Listen," put in Sept-Epées, "what you are telling me sounds like ingratitude. If you deserve friendship as you claim, why should I not give it to you! Inspire it in me, before you judge me incapable of being your friend."

"You are right, brave child," Audebert admitted, throwing his arm around the young man's shoulders. "Come, I will tell you everything. I will confess all to you, before God and the stars!"

CHAPTER V

When the two men had settled themselves outside, Audebert began his tale.

"At forty years of age, I could have remarried to some widow, especially since at that time the plague had left vacant spots in a good many households; but I was too grief-stricken over the loss of my own little family to consider such a thing, and I did not consider myself strong enough to love or be loved sufficiently to weather the hard work of being married. Living alone, at least one is spared most serious worries, and can focus on his own comfort. Our industries do well enough; the biggest problems come when there are too many mouths to feed.

"So, I stayed alone and miserable for several years, working hard to keep my mind off my troubles, and spending nothing, since I didn't have the heart to seek out song or dance. My money seemed to multiply by itself, and one day, when I was feeling a little less sad than I did on most others, I decided to do as your godfather did a little later; that is, to adopt an orphan and try to give him the happiness which I was no longer capable of feeling myself.

"This idea led me to think about the plight of the worker in general, because as I was searching the village for the orphan most deserving of my generosity I saw so many pitiable cases, perhaps even more among those children with parents than those without them, that I would have liked to be able to adopt all of them. After that I changed my plans and tried to find a way to improve this sad state of affairs.

"Thinking of those days still pains me. At first I thought I might try to found some sort of charitable association to help those in need, but it would have required a great deal of money to establish, and a strong initial effort. I possessed neither the funds nor the force of will to set up such an association on my own, nor did I have enough acquaintance among the wealthy to seek financial assistance, so I decided I would try to form an organization that would allow me to work for the good of everyone. I didn't yet know exactly what that might be, and I started so many projects to this end that it would be useless to try to recount them all—I did not have the money to complete any of them. I want to make it clear, my young friend, that it was not a desire for wealth that motivated me. It was the affinity I felt for all my fellow sufferers. I would have liked to put a chicken in the pot of every craftsman, as I have read King Henri IV did, and I was suddenly possessed by a strong sense of self-love, as if I had heard a voice in my head that said, 'Work, and believe in yourself! You have been chosen to be the father of the Black City!'

"That was my undoing, young one! I believed myself to be superior to other men, and I did not wish to bother with calculations because I was certain that destiny would provide for me. I poured all my assets into the venture, and I overspent—it takes patience to start a successful enterprise. I hired more workers than I needed and I soon found that I was burdened with a surplus of product I couldn't sell. My confidence fled, and I must tell you I didn't want to believe that with such a project, I could yet fail to find the generosity and assistance that I expected to encounter everywhere.

"I had placed too much faith in destiny, and now destiny itself abandoned me. One year I made a fair profit; it went to my head. I believed I was near the wealth I had dreamed of, and began to act as if it was already mine. I bought several parcels of land, with the goal of setting up some sort of idyllic farm.

"I saved nothing, and the money I had just earned barely covered my expenses. I carelessly took on more and more debt. When I finally realized how much money I had come to owe, I began to worry. I thought that once people heard my ideas for improving the working conditions in our town, ideas which I turned over and over in my head, I'd be surrounded by educated people who would help me to achieve my goals. I went to consult a very learned man in the Upper Town and asked him to participate in my plan—to help me frame my ideas properly and submit them to the proper authorities. This man was Monsieur Anthime, whose son recently became a doctor. He isn't rich, but he is quite well respected in these parts, as you must know.

"He listened to me patiently and attentively, but when I

tried to express my ideas clearly and logically I realized that I couldn't find the right terms. I had no trouble explaining the problems I saw around me or lamenting the suffering of the average craftsman, but when it came to offering the solution I had claimed to have, my thoughts became all mixed up and scrambled in my poor head, and I couldn't put them into words. It was apparently too late—I had already encountered too many difficulties.

"'My friend,' the good man I had consulted said to me, 'all of your confused ideas have already been thought of, written down, proposed, and discussed by men much more capable than you. We haven't yet resolved the problems of today's craftsman in such a way as to immediately better his condition, but we are still working on it. It's a worthy goal, but it is among the most difficult in the world. Addressing it effectively takes a great deal of study. I don't doubt your natural talent, but you know nothing of what passes ten leagues outside your Black City, or of the problems of today's society. You're wasting your time and energy without being of any help to anyone. You would be better off simply earning your living, and since I know that you are having a bit of trouble, I will be glad to help you in any way I can.'

"Foolishly, I refused my friend's offer of work. I was offended and discouraged at having been seen as an imbecile—I, who had believed myself so extraordinary! Like Napoleon to his St. Helena, I retired to the cliffs to ruminate, and there, contemplating the sky and the scenery around me, I felt all of my misplaced pride returning.

"Some mischievous demon was sporting with me. There, in

my solitude, I was filled with sublime ideas, and I could express them clearly, brilliantly! It was simply that all my aplomb deserted me the instant I tried to explain my thoughts to someone else. It took the scorn of one of my lowliest employees to show me the truth.

"One day I realized that no one contradicted me any longer—they simply turned away when they saw me, as if I were a criminal or a fool. Shame engulfed me, and with it a sense of despair so strong that I felt capable of any desperate action. Reason seemed to leave me entirely, and I came back to myself only after shedding many bitter tears.

"Then, my business went from poor to worse.

"I neglected my affairs completely. I was drowning in self-pity and despair. I found no respite from my misery, even in my dreams of saving mankind.

"What did it matter how much I had lost? What did it matter if I gave up? As long as I left behind my ideas for improving the lives of others, I would at least have done some good—this is what I told myself, but I couldn't find the secret of happiness for myself or anyone else.

"When I saw that my scant assets were about to be seized and myself probably clapped in debtor's prison, my eyes were finally opened to reality and I knew that my reasonable and logical friend in the Upper Town had judged me all too accurately. I went and asked him to help me with his signature, but it was too late—I had gravely offended him, and besides, he thought that letting me keep my factory would only encourage my folly. He again made me an offer of employment, which I could not bring myself to accept.

"After that, I thought of death often, and it soothed me. You see me thus calmed, my son, because I have decided to use suicide as my protest against the unfortunate hand that life has dealt me. People have called me ambitious and grandiose, a liar and a fool. They love nothing more than to kick a man when he is down. As God is my witness, I never meant any harm to anyone, and any mistakes I have made were a result of my own ignorance. As Monsieur Anthime said, 'Woe to the worker with too much imagination.' Then, too, there was the terrible pain of losing my wife and children in the space of eight days, a pain followed by the loneliness of a solitary existence I was not made to endure—it must have affected my mind. I was crazy, I admit it; I believe now that everyone has abandoned me, but I have always been honest. I wanted to help people from the bottom of my heart. I trusted people, and I believed in God, and in myself and others—and I was wrong. I do not wish to be a burden to anyone, nor a liar, and I would rather die than be useless, so I have decided to put an end to my sorry existence—tomorrow, if not today."

"I must say, you have quite a bad attitude," said Sept-Epées, after a few moments' thought as to what he might say to deter Audebert from his plan. "You will certainly never raise yourself in others' esteem that way; in fact, the opposite will happen. People will think your conscience tormented you, since everyone knows that a man with a clear conscience always has reason enough to continue living. In my opinion, killing yourself would be the worst sin of pride that you have committed so far—and the falsest of your illusions, because people would scorn your memory instead of grieving for you."

This admonitory statement seemed to make an impression on Audebert. "Scorn me?" he repeated. "Scorn? Surely people are not so callous that they will scorn a poor man for having the courage to kill himself!"

"It doesn't take any courage to kill yourself," returned Sept-Epées, "it is too quickly done! It takes a great deal more courage to live, and work."

"Too much courage!"

"So then, you do not possess enough?"

"Perhaps not! I don't wish to depend on others for my daily bread, after having hoped for so long that I might be the one to supply it to them."

"And what's the difference between taking bread from others and taking their money in exchange for providing a service? If it were the same thing, no one would be free; only thieves and loafers would be able to hold their heads up."

Sept-Epées, who had wisdom and judgment as well as a generous heart, continued to ply Audebert with phrases of wit and honesty, and he did this so well that the older man eventually promised that he would not consider another suicide attempt until he had taken three months to reflect upon its consequences. He had refused to swear by this promise before, but he swore by it now, and this was no small feat in view of his dejected state of mind.

"Since you are being a bit more reasonable now," continued Sept-Epées, "I would like to know what your factory is worth. I'll pay you more than its appraised value, and when your debts have been paid you will see all of your old friends return to your side."

"What? My poor child, do you mean that you wish to buy this rat trap?" cried Audebert. "No, no! I like you far too much to let you do that! It is badly situated, inhabited by the devil himself, and if my business could not succeed here, surely none will."

"Forgive me for saying so, but that is not a reason. You said yourself that you handled your affairs badly. Would you not like to do business with me? I would keep you on as overseer, and you will thus be able to chat from time to time with a friend who will never mock you. If, indeed, you were not able to solve the problems of humanity—as many a learned man has failed to do before you—then neither are you an ordinary man. I have listened to you speak with a great deal of pleasure, and I would certainly be the last person to criticize a man with a firm goal. I believe that gives you much more worth than those who have neither heart nor spirit."

"Finally—a kind word!" Audebert cried. "It does my poor soul more good than all your reasonable urgings put together! I accept your offer. I will work for you, and tomorrow we'll go together to the solicitor who is handling the liquidation of my assets. I will do everything I can to see that you get the factory at a good price without displeasing my creditors too much."

Sept-Epées was reluctant to let his new friend spend the night alone in the mountains. He feared a return of Audebert's hallucinations. The two men erased the sinister words written on the factory wall, and then went together to Laguerre's home in the Black City.

The young man planned to give Audebert his bed; being somewhat fastidious in his habits, he preferred to sleep on the floor rather than cramming two people into a bed meant for one, but Audebert refused the offer and, indicating Laguerre, who slept like a rock and snored like a furnace, said, "This will not be the first time he and I have shared a pallet. We were friends as boys. I know how soundly he sleeps, and I assure you that he won't even notice my presence."

In fact, Father Laguerre, rising before dawn as was his habit, was quite shocked to find someone asleep beside him. He concluded that Sept-Epées had drunk rather too much the night before and stumbled into the wrong bed upon returning home. Grumbling, he gave the intruder a shove toward the edge of the pallet. Audebert awoke. "What's this!" he cried indignantly. "I am not some dog who has jumped onto the bed; I am an old friend who would have offered you all of my goods, my hospitality, even my money if I had made my fortune! I have lost everything, but that is no reason to scorn me! Give me a handshake, and a little time to rouse myself before I leave."

"I see who it is," retorted Laguerre, furrowing his brow, "it is a man at the end of his rope, friendless, without a penny or a pillow upon which to lay his head, a bit like a lazy bird that has neglected to build his own nest and tries to benefit from the labor of others!"

Audebert seized his clothes and began dressing. "So, you chase me from your home as well! I should have expected this, and perhaps I did, a bit. Ah, what is one more slight when a man is miserable!"

"You are the one who humiliated and offended me!" roared Laguerre. "You forgot that I was your friend and let yourself fall into misery, as if you expected me to reject you! You are a fool with an enormous ego, and you do not deserve my forgiveness. If you leave this time, it will be finished forever between us."

Sept-Epées, hearing the quarrel from his bed, could not help laughing at his godfather's indignation. It was hardly the most effective tactic to use with Audebert, who had considerably more energy but far less reason than his friend. The two old men were on the point of tearing out what little hair remained to either of them, one demanding a handshake that the other refused to give until his offer of help was accepted.

"I know what you think of me and my thrift," exclaimed Laguerre, "you take me for an old miser who clutches his every penny, and you preferred to suffer the humiliation of bankruptcy when you knew full well that I would have loaned you any amount you wished if you had done me the simple courtesy of paying me a visit! But no, you have your pride! You thought yourself better than everyone else, and you mocked your elders—and I *am* your elder, sir! I am four years older than you, and despite my ignorance and my low position in life you owe me your respect! It was your responsibility to come to me, and not mine to come to you. Finally, here you are. You should be pitied for your foolhardiness! There is some money, sir, a whole drawer full of it! Yes, look there, the savings of a greedy fool! Take what you need and have the grace not to thank me—you came to me only when there was no one else left, and I don't need your pretty words. I don't want your friendship, and it has been a long time since I did!"

As he spoke, the old man, as proud of his frugality as his friend had once been of his prodigality, strutted half-clothed around the room, and, seizing the drawer filled with money, threw it to the floor where Audebert, offended by the manner in which it was offered, refused it with all the injured hauteur of an estranged brother.

CHAPTER VI

It was with difficulty that Sept-Epées calmed the old men and tried to reconcile their differences. He and Audebert had agreed to say nothing of the abortive suicide attempt, which would have disgusted Laguerre's austere and religious soul. As Audebert reddened with discouragement, Sept-Epées explained their encounter of the night before in such a manner as to make it appear deliberate on his part. Seeing an opportunity, he broached the subject of—and his ideas for—Audebert's little factory with his godfather.

"It would be impossible," he said, "for this brave man to accept your charity. His well-known pride would never allow that. Let him settle his debts by selling the factory, and allow him to be rehabilitated through work. I will take responsibility for helping him with both. If I don't succeed, I promise you, on his behalf, that he will come himself and seek your advice and friendship."

Audebert was grateful to Sept-Epées for his well-chosen words. Knowing the eccentric character of Laguerre as he did, he would not for the world have chosen to enter into his debt. In truth, he would rather have put his neck back into the noose.

Sept-Epées desperately wanted his godfather's assent to the project. If he refused it, the young man was quite able to finance it on his own, and he told himself that he would do so if need be, but he knew such an action would cause great pain to Laguerre, whom he loved tenderly. He told the older man as much in a few words, and succeeded in obtaining permission to undertake the new venture much more quickly than Audebert expected him to.

Laguerre sighed. "If this is truly what you wish to do, I don't have the right to stand in your way. What is yours, is yours. If you asked my opinion, I would tell you to keep what you have earned by the sweat of your brow in case you ever become ill or unable to work, and that it is always a comfort to have the means to help a friend or relative who can no longer help himself, but you are still so young that even if you lose your money, you will have the time to earn it back again. Besides, look at me—I am an old man, and what I've saved will come to you. It's not much, but it is a guarantee of a loaf of bread or two, and I don't think you will have to wait a hundred years for it! So, if you wish to take this risk, take it. You wish to open a factory by the river? Better that than a shop in the Upper Town! At least you will develop ties within our parish, and forget these ideas of moving away. Let us go then—don't waste the day repeating the same thing ten times over! What is decided, is decided. Go and see the solicitors, and since you will have to leave me, I'll begin looking for an apprentice to take your place. I'm too old to be here alone."

"Don't even think of such a thing," retorted Sept-Epées. "I have no intention of leaving you. The workshop isn't suitable for living in, and I would not wish you to undergo such a drastic change at your age. I have strong legs, and I can easily walk to work each day and return here at night. If the place earns me any money, I will sell it and buy one closer to home, where you can give me the benefit of your advice as often as I need it."

"And where I am not to intrude too often," smiled Laguerre. "I understand, and I approve. Each man must be king of his own castle. You will stay with me for the time being, and I'm glad of it. I still don't believe I will have the pleasure of your company for too much longer, but I will enjoy it as long as I can."

Two months passed while Sept-Epées established himself in the factory. The transaction had been concluded in a manner that pleased both him and Audebert. If Audebert had waited for his creditors to sell the building, it would certainly have lost too much value to be a significant asset to the buyer. The young smith showed a great deal of wisdom and good judgment in the affair, achieving his goal of a reasonable purchase price without taking advantage of his friend's misfortune. In so doing, he followed the advice of his godfather, who had a strong sense of honor and said that a bad reputation would never make a strong foundation for any workplace.

Audebert proved to be a useful associate. Since he no longer had to pour his energies into the ownership of the factory, he focused instead on renovating the building, and directed a large part of the operations himself. He moved back into the small apartment that he had previously occupied on the premises, so he could keep a watchful eye on things when his young partner had gone home each evening. The factory was soon back in operation, with new machinery and six hired workers—four part-time and two full-time.

When Sept-Epées had time to calculate the net earnings for each week, he was unpleasantly surprised to realize that they amounted to approximately half of what he would have earned working twelve hours a day for someone else. Ownership holds dreams of peace and security that a man must take for what they are worth; it cannot be denied that they provide the sweetness of hope—one cherishes an idea of perfection, and scorns any obstacle that may arise—but the realization of such dreams, like so much in reality, often involves cruel disappointment.

After a little time had passed, Sept-Epées realized that the more a man complicates his life, the more grief and danger he invites into it. He worried that he was not working efficiently enough to achieve the wealth he desired. He simply did not know how to sell his products aggressively. He granted extensive paid leave to sick or incapacitated workers. He launched sales efforts that returned too small a profit, or none at all. He began to doubt his abilities, and to believe that others would never understand the passion with which he pursued his goals. He found something lacking in everyone he came in contact with, and because he was sensitive and thoughtful, he began to fear that something was lacking in himself as well.

With his spirit thus abashed by doubt, he tried to improve the difficult situation in which he found himself by working harder and longer hours than he should. Sometimes he was so exhausted that he felt he had sold himself into a sort of slavery. Indeed, he felt truly bound by this project to which he had committed himself. It had become his honor, his life—he could not forget it for even one instant. Gaucher's prediction had come true: "You will know neither happiness nor pleasure." Gaucher had said those chilling words without fully understanding their import; Sept-Epées had heard them, and now he comprehended them completely. They echoed in his ears during the long hours of toil, but it was too late to turn back. He must try to ignore his regrets, and stifle his youthful restlessness.

The greatest of his worries was occasioned by the very man whose honor and life he had saved. Audebert, fired by the excitement of this new beginning, worked zealously and oversaw the workers with diligence during the first two or three weeks, but he soon fell back into the depression that had gripped him before, and his powerless state began to wear on him.

The first time he received a rebuke from his young employer, the poor man was profoundly wounded. Audebert was likable, sensitive, and overly delicate; he had all the qualities of a good heart and a virtuous soul, but he was one of those men of whom one might say, in comparing intellect to industriousness, that he did not possess the brain of a true work horse. Reviling himself for his faults, he missed three days of work, and Sept-Epées, observing

Audebert's discouragement, felt obliged to apologize for reprimanding him.

To be sure, the young man was failing to keep all the promises he had made. He had led Audebert to believe that he would be an attentive listener and sympathetic admirer of the older man's philosophical theories. He had convinced himself that there was a useful—indeed, noble—distraction in the conversation of this naive thinker, who was so eloquent in his own way and remained unfailingly positive in his vision, but he also knew all too well that it was impossible to listen too long to someone whose thoughts lacked clarity and focus. Audebert's way of thinking was too contradictory. Any paradox was acceptable to him as long as it supported his ideas, and he had become so entangled in the world of his dreams that he often did not hear the chimes of the clock summoning him to work. It was at these times that he should have let his long and vague discussions trail away and set himself aggressively to work, but his questionings persisted, and Sept-Epées had neither the time nor the patience to calm the doubts that constantly returned to plague the older man. The confused mixture of faith and bitterness that Audebert displayed repelled Sept-Epées's own innate logic. The older man's distracted manner and futile efforts to reconcile reality with his vision of a perfect life became like knife wounds to the younger man's heart. Audebert's overly sensitive nature caused him to see disdain and condemnation at every turn, a trait aggravated by the knowledge of his own incompetence. In truth, it was this last that worried Sept-Epées the most. Without telling Audebert,

Sept-Epées had spent several nights watching in less than hospitable weather over the deserted factory, out of fear that his unfortunate friend would give in to the temptation of suicide. The time Audebert had agreed to refrain from contemplating his inclination to kill himself had already elapsed, and Sept-Epées did not dare to ask him to commit to a longer period. He dreaded the possibility of failure in the event that he did ask, as he would thus be reminding Audebert of the fact that he was now theoretically free to end his own life.

Laguerre had come only once to visit his godson's enterprise. He disapproved but did not wish to lay blame. The young man had, naturally, adopted the newest operating techniques in his factory, and the older man, just as naturally, despite the experience age had brought him, was reluctant to concede that the new was better than the old. He did not believe that Sept-Epées would succeed, but he refrained from saying so, for he knew all too well that contradiction tends to stimulate obstinate minds. He confided in Gaucher, Lise, and several other old friends about his doubts, saying, "I don't hold out much hope; the place is badly situated, and if the boy can cut his losses after five or six years of toil it will be a lesson well worth learning. At least, it may teach him to content himself in the future with what satisfies the rest of us. After all, with all his ambition, I would rather he make this mistake than that of leaving the Black City altogether. When I see other fools spend every cent they have so that they can pretend to be a bourgeois citizen on Saturday nights, frittering away their time in the taverns of the

Painted Trap (for that was how Laguerre referred to the Upper Town), drinking and playing at billiards, just to return on Tuesday morning bedraggled and exhausted, spouting here and there a new word acquired among the snobs, I think that my boy is a great deal more intelligent than all of them. I am thankful that I was able to teach him, in spite of his resistance to my guidance, the desire and ability to succeed in his chosen field through honest means, for that lesson learned marks him truly as a member of our parish."

Gaucher had optimistically shared in the dreams of his young friend. He was himself possessed of a youthful and idealistic spirit, and his confidence in the abilities of others made him an agreeable and supportive companion. The selfless interest he took in his friends' successes served as a temporary distraction from the unvarying toil of his own daily routine.

"Bah!" he exclaimed to his wife when she tried to convince him that he had more reason to be happy than Sept-Epées did. "A man is always happy when he is doing what he loves! My pleasure is to work and live for you, and if my friend has different ideas, he is more than welcome to follow them! We must not discourage him; indeed, we must be ready to help him—whatever he may ask of us."

One spring Sunday, four months into his ownership, Sept-Epées, returning from several selling trips that had not been as successful as he had hoped they might, closeted himself in the factory. It was his habit to spend Sundays in the Black City with his godfather and his friends; however, Audebert was ill and could not leave his room, so Sept-Epées had remained to care for his sick friend.

He decided to take advantage of the quiet of the day to look over the factory's books, which he believed to be in good order. He was quite adept at calculations, but his active nature tended more toward manual labor and the transacting of business than to poring over accounts. Audebert was a passable accountant, and much better at looking after the affairs of others than at conducting his own. During the first three months he had fulfilled the task admirably, but when Sept-Epées examined the books for the fourth month he found ample evidence that the older man's mind had wandered, as he had categorized a number of figures as profits that were actually expenditures. It was as if a fever, or some sort of delusion, had overtaken him as he sat working and had caused him to lose his train of thought completely. The mistakes would not be easy to repair, and Sept-Epées realized that he could not rely on his friend's lucidity any longer. He told himself wryly that from now on he would have to do everything by himself. Still, he had no wish to trouble his friend during his illness by pointing out his mistakes. Then, since he had been away all week, he decided to inspect the factory's machinery and tools.

Sept-Epées found the same lack of order on the factory floor that he had in the account books. Even the principal generator was out of service, after an accident that had gone unreported to him. An expensive repair would be needed as soon as possible to avoid a shutdown of one or even two weeks. He would have to hurry into town to find a specialist who could come the next day. However, when he mentioned the mishap to Audebert, the older man responded by saying blearily that his head was as broken as the generator. He was clearly delirious with fever, and Sept-Epées became worried. He had asked his workers to send a doctor the night before, and they had either forgotten or the doctor was reluctant to make the journey to such an inhospitable location; in any case, no one had come, and the sick man's condition worsened by the hour.

The situation was aggravated by a terrible storm that descended on the area. The wind howled in the gorge, and the river, swelling with alarming rapidity, threatened to engulf the factory. A sinister cracking sound ran along the cliffs, then a deluge of stones and gravel that pummeled the roof of the building—a heavier fall would surely destroy it. When the wind finally quieted down, so did Audebert; or, rather, his fevered ranting turned to melancholy and tears. His fragile nerves irritated by the chilly air and the sound of the rain pounding the windows, he was seized by a primitive terror, and dissolving in tears, he repeated again and again the old refrain—that the building was haunted, possessed by the devil himself.

Sept-Epées did his best to fortify the factory against the ever-rising river by improvising artificial barriers to protect the precious equipment from the rushing tide. Working alone, at the risk of his life, he displayed energy that was nearly superhuman. The pleas and sobs of Audebert, still audible over the roaring water and pealing thunder, drove him to a sort of rage; despite himself, he felt that the old man's negativity was threatening to overwhelm his own determination. He tried in vain to drown out Audebert's cries with his own oaths. He yelled again and again for his friend to seek shelter in the upper gallery, which was protected from the flood, but Audebert did not understand, and Sept-Epées, beginning to despair of saving his property, considered carrying his recalcitrant companion bodily down the mountain.

Sept-Epées tried desperately to force one last plank into the barrier that he hoped would save his factory from the surging water. The plank obstinately refused to fit, and Sept-Epées, struggling, plied to it with all his strength. Finally, with a supreme effort, he wrestled the board into place. Just at that moment, his feet slipped on the wet stone, and he would have tumbled into the river if it had not been for the timely appearance of a steadying hand, which, grasping his own, pulled him to drier ground. The rain, beginning to subside, battered with less violence against the factory's sodden foundation.

Everything was saved. Sept-Epées, who had himself been rescued from almost certain death, turned to see who had so fortuitously come to his aid—and froze with shock when he recognized Tonine Gaucher.

CHAPTER VII

It had been some time since Sept-Epées had seen Tonine face to face. Occasionally he had passed her on the street when he returned to the Black City in the evenings, and on Sundays, when he went to visit Gaucher, he had sometimes heard her leave the room by one door as he entered by another. She'd seemed to be avoiding him, and for his part, his guilt regarding her had compelled him not to speak to her.

Now, of course, he was obliged to greet her, and to thank her, and to ask how she came to be there at that precise moment.

"By the greatest coincidence in the world," she replied, stepping inside the shelter of the factory and shaking out her rain-drenched cloak. "I started out when the weather was still fair, taking the high road to visit my former nanny in the Upper Town, but the storm took me by surprise. I sought shelter under an overhanging rock, and I would be there still if a doctor had not passed by and offered me a ride in his carriage. He told me he first had a visit to make, but then he would take me to the Upper Town. That seemed better than staying where I was! As we continued along the way, he indicated that he was coming down to see a sick man, and since he had never been here before, he didn't know the road to the bottom of the gorge. I came down with him to show him the way, and the terrain was so treacherous that we decided to wait for the storm to die a bit—and here we are. The doctor is with your friend Audebert now. I didn't think to see you, since you usually spend Sundays in town—or so I'm told—and I thought I would come and see if there was someone looking after that poor man. That is when I saw you and the river, locked in combat."

"And if it were not for you, Tonine, I think I might well have lost the battle."

"Oh, no! If you were really going to fall, my poor strength would certainly not have saved you!"

"Ah, but it was your noble heart that gave me the strength to save myself."

"A noble heart does not prevent a man from drowning! You would have saved yourself from the water even if I had not happened by. I remember when we were children, and you and my cousin got into mischief all over town."

"You remember our childhood together, Tonine? I thought you had forgotten me completely, and I must say I would deserve it if you had."

"Come, let us not speak of that now," said Tonine quickly. "Go and see to your poor old friend, who may not know what to tell the doctor."

"Will I find you here when I return, Tonine?"

"My goodness—of course! It is not exactly the weather to be out picking daisies!"

"Let me at least stoke the furnace so that you can get warm. It will only take a moment."

Sept-Epées lit the fire without waiting for Tonine's response, then climbed the stairs to the upper story of the building, where Audebert languished in his sickroom.

"This man is not well," said the doctor quietly on seeing Sept-Epées, "and it won't be easy to heal him. Medicine must be fetched from the Upper Town as soon as possible, and he must be made to take it—he gives me the impression of being stubborn when it comes to accepting medical aid."

Sept-Epées had no one to send into town for the medicine, and he was reluctant to leave his friend alone. He asked the doctor to return to town by himself, and then send a courier with the medicine.

"That will take too long," Tonine interjected, having followed the young smith upstairs. "It's Sunday, and poor weather, too. You may not find anyone willing to deliver the medicine. Go yourself, Sept-Epées, and I'll stay here with the invalid."

"No—you should not; he is delirious with fever."

"Not at all," she responded, touching Audebert's arm. "In fact, I believe his fever has broken. Don't worry, we understand each other quite well. Isn't that right, Father Audebert?"

"And who are you, my girl?" the old man inquired, coming back to his senses a bit. "Oh, yes—the sister of poor Suzanne Molino. Yes, you're right, my dear. I wouldn't wish to be any trouble for you. We have both suffered enough in this life, you and I."

"You see," Tonine said to Sept-Epées, "you should go. Doctor Anthime can get you to town quickly. His horse is wonderfully fast."

"Anthime?" cried Audebert, who, as if by magic, had recovered his lucidity since Tonine entered the room. "You, my good doctor, are the son of an admirable man to whom I have been most profoundly ungrateful. Please give him my apologies, and my very best wishes."

When Sept-Epées and Anthime had begun their journey into town, the young doctor questioned the other man about Tonine. "I remember the marriage of her sister to Molino," he said. "Tonine must have been a child then. I have been away from home ever since; I studied medicine in Paris. When I returned I found that I no longer knew anyone in the area. It was by chance I met that young woman on my way to see you. I must admit I was quite impressed by her speech and her graceful manners. Is she not married, then? She must have a suitor, at least; all the young women working in the Black City do, it seems. Or—is she engaged?" He trailed off uncertainly, seeing Sept-Epées' involuntary frown.

The young smith replied coldly that Tonine was very intelligent, and well respected by everyone who knew her.

"That doesn't surprise me," Anthime mused. He roused himself and, turning to the subject of Audebert, asked a few questions about the old man's medical history, but he soon resumed his inquiries about Tonine. "She spoke to you in a friendly manner—have you known her long?" Sept-Epées kept his answers as short and noncommittal as he could, and the subject was finally dropped, but when Anthime dropped him off at the apothecary's, the doctor added one final thing. "There should be a woman caring for your friend Audebert. Try and see that Tonine stays at his bedside—she has a soothing manner. I'll come and see him again after the midday meal."

Sept-Epées was so preoccupied by the effect Tonine had obviously had on the young doctor that he completely forgot to tell Gaucher of her whereabouts as she had requested. He thought only of returning from the apothecary's with the medicine as soon as he could.

He hastened back to the factory and found Tonine seated at Audebert's bedside, chatting comfortably. The old man's fevered agitation had fled completely. Tonine convinced him to take the medicine he had sworn to refuse, and to take it without the slightest complaint. "I have caused you a great deal of trouble, my poor boy," he said, taking the hands of his young master. "I was out of my mind with fever, and I'm sure you were at a loss as to what to do—but God has sent us an angel, and Tonine's words were a calming medicine in themselves. I believe she possesses more strength of spirit than you and I together! See how we can spend years as neighbors, and yet never know one another! Tonine, if you wish me to try and sleep, you must promise to be here when I wake."

Tonine promised Audebert that she would stay, and asked Sept-Epées if he had told Gaucher where she was. He was about to confess that he had forgotten, when Gaucher saved him the trouble by arriving himself. The rising water had caused him to worry about his young friend, and he had come to check on the condition of the factory. He was surprised to see his cousin there, but after everything had been explained to him he turned his attention to the problem of repairing the damage the storm had done. With characteristic generosity, he offered to go into town and fetch men to help them restore the factory to working order, but Tonine held him back. She had promised not to leave Audebert, and she asked her cousin to keep her company while Sept-Epées went back home to reassure his godfather that all was well and then to inquire in town after the workers himself.

Sept-Epées was troubled. Some new thought was stirring in his mind. The damage to his factory, which he had felt to be so important this morning, now hardly seemed worthy of his attention—but he did not dare ask Gaucher to go into town in his stead, as he was certain that Tonine had no desire to find herself alone with him while Audebert slept.

He returned to town, stopped briefly to see his godfather, and then gathered his employees, who surveyed the damage to the factory and promptly set to work. This project, naturally, occupied the remainder of the day, and he did not have a chance to see Tonine, who remained upstairs with Audebert. When the workers had gone for the day, Sept-Epées realized that he had not taken the time to eat or drink anything, and since he had spent the previous night watching over his friend and had taken very little rest, he suddenly felt quite weak. Gaucher called for Tonine, who got him to swallow down a bit of soup. The factory was decently stocked with the necessary provisions, but the young apprentice in charge of cooking did not usually work on Sundays, and he was in no hurry to interrupt his single day of rest. He finally arrived toward evening, as did the doctor. The sick man had slept peacefully and was feeling a great deal better. Sept-Epées was touched by Tonine's generosity and fortitude. Doctor Anthime, he noticed, looked at her often.

"You don't have to stay here," Gaucher, who had witnessed the doctor's glances as well, hastened to assure Anthime. "We can manage for the night." He turned to Sept-Epées. "As for you, my young friend, you are obviously on your last legs. You should go to your godfather's house and sleep. I'll stay here and keep watch over Audebert. The cook will be here if I need anything. We can all meet tomorrow—there's no need for anyone to die of fatigue."

"And who will take me back to town?" interjected Tonine.

"I will," Anthime said quickly. "My carriage is outside, on the high road."

"But she doesn't live in the Upper Town," put in Sept-Epées with a firmness that did not go unnoticed by Gaucher.

"I know it. I'll take her around to the Black City."

"That will take too long," Gaucher said in a tone of quiet complicity. "You mustn't trouble yourself."

The young doctor, realizing that Tonine's cousin did not intend to entrust her to him, turned to leave. She followed him to the door to ask him one more time for the names of the medicines that Gaucher was to give Audebert during the night. He seized the opportunity to speak to her, and asked if she was afraid to go with him.

"No," the girl replied, "I do not consider myself pretty enough to be in danger around any man."

"Oh! And is that your only reason?"

"If that is not reason enough, here is another one. I do not deserve to be admired by one such as yourself—though I do thank you for your politeness. I do not consort with the middle class. You know very well that it isn't suitable for a factory worker's daughter."

Anthime gazed at her. "And would you feel safer if Sept-Epées took you home?"

"I would certainly feel myself safer from gossip."

Gaucher, uncomfortable with the length and direction of the conversation, interrupted them. "The girl is right. She may go with one of her own class—and that does not include someone like you, sir."

Anthime looked defeated. "I understand," he said quietly, and withdrew.

"Indeed!" Tonine exclaimed indignantly to her cousin when they were alone. "That isn't what I meant! I do not trust anyone—it has nothing to do with class."

"Is that so?" returned Gaucher. "You could have trusted Sept-Epées, and you did not want him."

"Oh, yes—I'd forgotten that," she said, forcing a laugh.

Sept-Epées, who had tried to listen in without being noticed, was both hurt and embarrassed by her gaiety. He would not have dared to offer to drive Tonine home, had Gaucher not said, "Come, we must not wait until it's completely dark. The road is not at its best, and some areas are surely still quite wet."

"Wait, cousin," Tonine put in. "I must write down a list of the medications for Audebert. I'm sure you will forget them otherwise."

Sept-Epées handed her one of his account books, and watched her write. He noticed the swiftness and elegance of her handwriting. "You would make a good bookkeeper," he remarked, smiling.

"As good as any man," she responded, "and my figures would certainly be neater than those already written here! Are these your scribbles?"

Sept-Epées replied with some satisfaction that they were Audebert's.

Tonine went to say good night to the old man, who had promised that he would submit to her ministrations as meekly as a kitten. While she was upstairs, Gaucher turned to Sept-Epées. "Well, my friend, if you are still interested in Tonine, now is your chance to change her thinking about you. Speak to her with all the charm I know you possess. Show her that you care for her, and perhaps she'll see you with new eyes."

"I cannot hope for that," Sept-Epées said. "She seems to have nothing but disdain for me."

"She has never said a single word against you to us," Gaucher assured him. "She simply told Lise and me that she did not wish to marry. It's your responsibility to change her mind, if you still wish to."

When Sept-Epées and Tonine had closed the factory

door behind them, he summoned all of his courage and faced the girl. "Tonine, my friend, you are indeed an angel, as Audebert said. I hope I can see you again. Without your sweet heart and your spirit, I would have lost the respect of my best friend. I was a fool; I behaved terribly toward you. I am sorry, and I've berated myself a hundred times. If I had dared, I would have asked your pardon the day after our last conversation."

"Why do you speak of these things now?" asked Tonine. "I accept your apology—if indeed you ever had anything to apologize for, which I do not believe to be the case."

"But I did! I courted you, and I was suddenly afraid to get married. I wanted to wait two or three years, until I could offer you a more secure life. But now, Tonine, since you have forgiven me—"

"Now, what?"

"Now that I am better established in my profession, though I am not yet where I aim to be, if you feel as brave as I do, now, Tonine. . . ."

"Brave enough to start a life with you?" said Tonine, seeming to force out the words. "No, my dear friend, I will never be brave enough to marry for bravery's sake. I am foolish enough to dream of happiness, friendship, and trust. I don't see that in you, but I do not blame you for it. The time for passion is past. You cannot offer me a secure life, as you call it. When your career is in order, perhaps I can hope to build a future with you. You will, I imagine, have consulted me when making your decisions, and we will have set up a life pleasing to both of us. Today, things are far from certain. You have bought a property that is worth close to nothing, in a place that might not be agreeable to me. You have not yet made up all you spent. How can you hope to support a wife and children? That would indeed be a burden for you. A year of poor sales, several weeks out of work, a flooding of the riverbank, and you could be brought to your knees. No sensible woman would entrust her security to you now."

Sept-Epées struggled with his mortification. "It seems to me that you have reason and sense enough for a hundred women, my lovely Tonine. You are right, but I must contradict one thing you said—it seems to me that friendship has no place in your marriage plans."

"I have no marriage plans," she replied. "I have nothing except my youth and my health, and I do not need anyone to earn my keep for me. I live as I choose. I keep to myself, alone in my room with a book on Sundays, or with other people's children in my lap. I do nothing I might regret the next day. If I become ill, it will be my own misfortune. If I die, I will not leave a grief-stricken family behind, and I will die peacefully, as one should when one is not needed by anyone. You must see that I have no reason to trade my life as it is for the one you're offering me."

"You are right, Tonine—so right, in fact, that there's nothing further to say. You do not love anyone. You care only for yourself; the happiness or sadness of others means nothing to you. Your life will be free from worry, and I must admit that you are indeed in control of your own existence!"

"I think, Sept-Epées, that you are condemning me, but it isn't your place to do so. You were quite as reasonable as I when you said that when a man marries, he loses his identity and the ability to change his life for the better, and that it's better to stay a single man and to seek one's own fortune. I have nothing to seek. I'm content to remain just as I am."

"I understand," Sept-Epées said in unconscious imitation of Doctor Anthime. "You are worth far too much to be easily won—and perhaps you are waiting for a greater fortune than I can provide!"

Tonine laughed. "If wealth finds me, then no one can criticize me for seeking it."

Sept-Epées was silent. He walked on, trying to conceal the pain he felt at Tonine's indifference.

CHAPTER VIII

Tonine and Sept-Epées came to a curve in the road where the water had collected to form a deep and impassable pool. Sept-Epées, observing that Tonine was preparing to skirt the water without his help, could not help but comment, with a smile, "Do you hate me so much, Tonine, that you will not allow me to do you even the smallest service? I may not be able to get us both across the water with dry shoes myself, but I do have two strong arms and I can see to it that your shoes remain safe."

"I'm too big to be carried like a little child," said Tonine, "and I won't die of wet feet."

"You don't want me to carry you?" Sept-Epées felt sudden anger overtake him. "Walk, then, if you want to!" He glared as she gathered up her skirts to cross the water, but when he saw her hesitate his exasperation deserted him, and swiftly he seized her up in his arms and carried her the twenty or thirty feet to dry land.

She looked at him, puzzled. "What is the matter with you, Sept-Epées? I felt your hot tears fall on my arm. Why do I upset you so much? Wait—let me tell you why. I believe you have convinced yourself that you are sorry you rejected me, because I took my leave without storming or weeping at you, but—if I were your wife now, you'd be sorry for that. Don't mistake pride for friendship—they are not at all the same."

"If you were my wife now," retorted Sept-Epées, "instead of feeling troubled and discouraged as I did when I saw you this morning, I would have someone to comfort me and give me hope. I don't think I would have been nearly so terrified when the river started to rise, or so angry at Audebert in his delirium. Tonine, I am so much unhappier than you know! I'm plagued by worry that I might fail in this enterprise, and expose myself to the ridicule of those who find me presumptuous and insolent for undertaking such a serious project at my age. I have assumed responsibility for a half-crazy old man whose friendship brings me more grief than pleasure. I spend hours—whole days—alone in that godforsaken factory. I tell you, Tonine, there are times when I could almost—"

The young man broke off without finishing his thought. He and Tonine did not speak for a moment. Finally, Tonine broke the silence. "It pains me to hear you talk like that, Sept-Epées, honestly it does—but you speak only of regretting your project. You haven't said that you regret not marrying, and if you were married and your business affairs took a turn for the worse, you would be even more miserable. My friend, you don't have a very soft heart, but you are an honest man. You would not—you could not lie. Admit it—during the four months that you have owned your factory, you have hardly thought of me at all."

"You are wrong, Tonine. I have thought of you a great deal, and often with sadness."

"Because you believed you had caused me pain. Tell the truth—you will not make me angry."

"All right; yes, I believed I had hurt you."

"I know that you have a good heart," said Tonine, "but if you could have looked into my heart and seen that I was truly not suffering, would you have said to me, as I have often heard my cousin Gaucher say to his wife, 'My dear, whether you love me or not, I know that I couldn't do without you'? Don't answer me lightly, Sept-Epées. I don't want you to be gallant and protect me. I want you to be completely honest."

Sept-Epées struggled with his thoughts for a moment. "I will admit that I have been so occupied with my worries that I have not had the time to think of anything else. My ambition has not extinguished my love, but it has indeed caused me to make mistakes. There—that is my confession. Is mine an unforgivable crime?"

"Certainly not; in fact, I think I could forgive you more readily now, if you truly loved me. Sincerity is a wonderful quality in my eyes, but you do not love me any more today than you did yesterday, my friend."

"I find you—"

"You find me more desirable now because I happened upon you at a moment of extreme difficulty and danger, and one always feels a need to reach out at times such as those. You also saw someone else paying attention to me, and your ego was threatened. Finally, you mistook my friendliness toward you for love. All of this has gone to your head, I am afraid. But now the danger has passed, and your worry will pass as well. No one loves me, and I do not love anyone. If you asked me to marry you this evening, you would regret it tomorrow, and I would regret having believed words of love which were not true."

"Enough," cut in Sept-Epées. "You are punishing me for my mistakes, and you want to kill me with the arrow that pierced your own heart! Well, you certainly have the right to do so. Is wealth to be my consolation? I'm beginning to lose my faith in it! I must have been out of my mind to stake so much happiness on something so uncertain."

Tonine shook her head. "You cannot give up so easily. You have made your bed and now you must lie in it. You must not be so discouraged when you have hardly begun. You would not be a man if you turned back at the first sign of difficulty; besides, if you change your ideas every day you will not inspire confidence in anyone. It is unfortunate, perhaps, that you have sacrificed your youth to ambition, and the present to the future, but it would be even worse to abandon this future for which you have already paid such a high price because of a few misfortunes that will pass as everything does. I'll return tomorrow morning to see the invalid as I promised, and we'll speak to Gaucher about all this."

"You will return to the factory tomorrow? At what time?"

"I don't know, but I don't want to go with you, Sept-Epées. It would cause too much talk, and even now we would do better to return to town separately. I will see you tomorrow, I promise. I hope you will think about everything very carefully, as a reasonable man should do, and try to keep a clear head."

Sept-Epées looked exasperated. "Why should you care if my head is clear, Tonine? You've said that you feel no love for me."

"There is love, and then there is love! There is a love where neither person can live without the other, and the two marry. You never had that sort of love for me, and I am relieved to say that I never had it for you, either. But there is also a calmer sort of love, where one person takes an interest in the affairs of another, and they are friends. At this point in our relationship, Sept-Epées, that is the most we can hope for, and I would like to share it with you. It does not have to be a matter of passion. You can act toward me just as you would toward Gaucher, or Lise. If this idea pleases you, we can begin to spend time together again. If it doesn't, then when you see me tomorrow it will be for the last time."

"I'll be whatever you like, Tonine, your husband or your brother, your lover or your friend. As long as we can be something to each other, I will be a great deal happier than I have been these past six months."

The following day, Sept-Epées satisfied Tonine by appearing at work with his employees and showing a carefree face to the world. Inside, however, he counted the hours and minutes until she arrived in the company of Lise and her two children. After the women had spent time with Audebert, who was much improved and had awaited Tonine's visit impatiently, Lise took her husband aside.

"There's something you need to know," she said.

"Tonine told me on the way here that your young friend is on the verge of despair and may abandon his plans if you do not help him. Why could you not spend a week or two working for him? The little ones and I would be sorry not to see you during the day, but after all, one cannot be completely selfish in this world. Audebert means well, but he won't be able to work for several days at least—and anyway, he is not the best person to be a companion to someone like Sept-Epées, as Audebert is well aware himself. He's even thinking of leaving here. If he does, you will be indispensable to Sept-Epées while he looks for another manager."

"I have already thought of that," admitted Gaucher, "but I didn't want to offer him my help without first speaking to you. You have never steered me wrong, my dear Lise, and since you have suggested it, then I will give credit for the idea to you. Talk to Sept-Epées, and tell him that if he wishes it, I'm at his service for the rest of the month."

Sept-Epées gratefully accepted his friend's generosity. Tonine came downstairs just then and approached him. "Yesterday I had the poor manners to laugh at your account books. If I had known then what Audebert has just told me, I would never have teased you about such a serious matter."

"What on earth can you be talking about?"

"He told me of several errors he remembers making, now that his fever has broken. He is afraid that you might not have noticed them, and he asked me to correct them. Would you allow me to see the books again, in spite of my joking yesterday?"

Sept-Epées smiled. "I'm well aware that the books are in disarray, but I promise you that I won't reproach Audebert. When my mind is a little more at ease, I'll try to untangle the mess he has made."

"Why not now?" inquired Tonine. "One should never put off until tomorrow what can be done today. You won't be able to work until all of your equipment is in order again, so why not let me help you this afternoon? We can surely straighten this out if we work together. Sit down there, and we'll put things to rights."

Tonine took up a pen and began transcribing Audebert's scribbled figures into a new register while, at the same time, checking each item with Sept-Epées. They soon found that despite the young man's efforts, the factory was not doing as well as it might.

Gaucher, who had been quite impressed with the project, was shocked to learn that its performance was so mediocre, though the factory was not as hopeless a failure as some jealous voices in the village claimed. Sept-Epées was relieved to speak openly of his business affairs at last, something he had not dared to do before, even with his closest friends. When a worker ascends the ladder of success and launches upon a business of his own, he assumes such immense responsibility that he is sometimes gregarious and self-satisfied, sometimes tight-lipped and wary. The young smith, who had been all of these by turns, finally felt comfortable. He reminded himself that a worry shared is a worry halved, when the worry is shared with a friend.

He turned to Tonine. "Now that you have helped me see

how things really are, can't we at least speak to each other in the village?"

"When I see you with an eye as clear as Gaucher's and a step as firm, then I will speak to you as I speak to him, but if I see you with a worried face and furrowed brows, as you have had during these last three months, I will cross to the other side of the street without saying anything other than hello. I don't wish to spend time in the company of people who act as if the entire world is against them. Now I want to return to the matter at hand: you must watch over Audebert tonight, as will Lise and I tomorrow night, and after us Gaucher, then you again. This way, he will mend quickly, as he has already begun to do, and once he has recovered fully he will leave your employ and come to work in town. He promised me this, and you must see that he does it. He spends too many nights here alone, and that isn't good for as fragile a soul as his; nor is it doing you any good. You need a younger man to help you oversee things here, and I believe I can recommend a good candidate. I think you should hire Va-sans-Peur—he is nicknamed 'Fearless' for good reason."

Sept-Epées shook his head. "Va-sans-Peur is not looking for work."

"But he is. He had an argument with his overseer yesterday, and I spoke to him this morning about coming to work here. He cannot read or write, but he has a good memory and a clear head. In the evenings, instead of returning to town at sunset, you can spend an extra hour at your desk. This way, you will always know the precise state of your affairs, and that will serve you a great deal better than the occasional glance you give the books now."

"Yes, doubtless it will. But what of my poor old godfather? He goes to bed early and does not like to eat supper alone."

Tonine smiled. "I believe it's the old housekeeper who nags him into retiring at such an early hour. She prepares supper at the same time every night, even if you are not there. He has complained to me about it many times. He says that if he stayed at the same boarding house as I do, he would be pleased to have my company in the evenings. If the idea is all right with you, I would be happy to arrange things, and the old gentleman will be well taken care of."

"Tonine," Sept-Epées said, laughing, "you are the smartest and most wonderful girl in the world! You could soften even the most stubborn heart. My godfather has been complaining for years about the house he lives in and the people who cook for him, and this may be the perfect time to suggest a change. I suppose I shouldn't be so surprised—only yesterday I was out of my mind with worry, and today my head is in the clouds! Why not? If my godfather lives in the same house as you, I will see you every day."

"Yes," replied Tonine, "but only as a brother, and a friend. There is nothing else between us! The more I see of how complicated life can be, the more reluctant I am to change my own. I am better off alone."

Tonine left Sept-Epées full of courage and hope. Whatever she might say to him, he felt confident that she would soon forgive him completely for their past differences. His self-esteem soared, and to his handsome face and intelligent mind he was at last able to add a carefree spirit. His happiness increased when Gaucher approached him and insisted that Tonine cared for him more than she would admit—or so he had been told by Lise, he said, and Lise was never wrong.

Just a few days later, Father Laguerre was settled in a comfortable room next to a chamber that had been appointed for Sept-Epées. The rooms were close to Tonine's at the Laurentis boarding house, run by a respectable and decent woman. Tonine had arranged with the proprietress to oversee the transfer of Laguerre's and Sept-Epées's things from their former home to their new one. Laguerre's thrift and Sept-Epées's carelessness had resulted in quite a shabby collection of possessions. Lise helped to remedy the situation, and one fine evening Sept-Epées was shocked to come home to a room filled with furnishings that seemed to be new again. Small tears had been mended, and everything had been cleaned and polished. Their modest supper was served on dishes without cracks, and Laguerre declared that the wine tasted better when drunk from a clean glass. It was quite a departure from their former situation, and the old man embraced it with vigor. He had never forgiven his former landlady for chasing off a cat of which he was particularly fond, after she'd caught it nosing through her pantry. In addition, Laguerre was simply enchanted by Tonine, who had had no trouble at all convincing him that it was time to make a change. Dropping by his home one morning to inquire after his health and give him the latest news of Audebert's condition, she had asked how such a dignified and distinguished old man had come to live in such slovenly conditions.

"It is surely the negligence of the people looking after you that has caused your reputation as a miser," she had said. "It would take only a little attention from those around you, I'm sure, to give you quite the air of a master craftsman, as indeed you are, and one of the most respected men in town. You deserve to live in comfort. If you roomed with Madame Laurentis as I do, you would never spend a Sunday with holes in the knees of your trousers and a shirt black with the soot of a week spent at the forge."

"The truth," the old man had responded, "is that the woman who looks after me now is good for nothing except killing cats, and I would be only too happy to show her that I can live a great deal more comfortably under a roof other than hers—and just as cheaply, too."

Sept-Epées suddenly found himself in another world. Instead of the sty he had shared with his godfather, he was living in a clean and quiet room from which he had a good view of their little town, with its paradoxical mix of smoke-stacks and sparkling waterfalls, coal and diamonds, bustling workers and tranquil pastures. Without fully understanding the poetry of his surroundings, he felt a sense of joy and well- being.

The daily life of a manufacturer is not always a pleasant thing. Few sights appear grimmer than that of a dim factory with its crew of employees, black with soot and drooping with fatigue, each bent over his work like a cog in some great machine, unaware of the passage of time, or indeed of anything except noise and smoke. When, however, this formidable machine is seen within the greater context of the outside world, and when an active and industrious population takes up the battle cry against inertia and its roar of victory over the elements is echoed by a thousand voices, the soul cannot help but soar. The heart thrills as if to the pounding of a drum, and it seems that all the force and power of the material world have been brought into play by the intellect of man, in a divine celebration of human triumph.

CHAPTER IX

Tonine may not have had a definite grasp of the intricately choreographed dance between man and machine, but she sensed it instinctively. This pale and delicate worker's daughter loved her Black City. She breathed as easily among its dark and narrow streets and alleyways as along the breezy banks of the river. She seemed to magically bring a bit of sunlight and fresh air into the lives of those she regarded as friends—and as she well knew, life is better in the light than in the depths of a cave.

Another pleasant change in Sept-Epées's life occurred when Va-sans-Peur came to work at his factory in place of Audebert, whom Tonine had been able to persuade to fill a vacant position in one of the workshops in town.

These changes had not been made without significantly affecting Audebert's emotional well-being. His pride as an ex-owner and partner in an independent enterprise did not easily accommodate his new, more humble status of worker and friend. He had realized that he was becoming a burden to Sept-Epées, but the idea of returning to the village seemed to him to hold the threat of scorn and renewed servitude.

Tonine, chatting with him, had discovered the secret of his wounded vanity—and a way to soothe it as well.

Audebert had failed to recognize one of his true talents—he was a poet. He had a way with the written word that was often lacking when he spoke, and he had the ability to endow his verse with color and life. He dreamed of an ideal world, and his nature was especially sensitive to the small dramas of a worker's existence. His mistake had been to believe that he could right the wrongs he saw every day in a world too hard-bitten for his altruistic spirit.

It was by chance that, during a mild recurrence of his fever, he began speaking in verse to Tonine. The phrases were not without grammatical errors, but they were musical and pleasing to the ear. They evoked vivid imagery and sincere emotion. When Audebert's fever had passed, Tonine asked him if he had ever written any songs.

"Yes, sometimes, to amuse myself," was the reply, "but I have never shown them to anyone. I would be ashamed to call myself a poet—there is nothing more tiresome! Poets do nothing but whine about their misfortunes without ever seeking a remedy for them."

"Nevertheless, I would be honored if you showed me your songs," said Tonine. "If you have never bothered to write them down, try to remember one or two now. Your poor head is too tired at the moment for you to spend much time thinking about your problems, which I don't completely understand anyway. A song would calm your nerves, and it would make me very happy."

Audebert consented to sing a few of his verses, and

Tonine and Lise found them quite pleasing indeed. They quickly committed them to memory and began singing them around town, where they were soon very popular. Audebert had been deprived of compliments for so long that he received with immeasurable pleasure those that were relayed to him by Tonine. The poor man had a tender heart to equal his sense of pride, and he desired love as much as he did admiration. He spent his convalescence out in the countryside, composing songs that became increasingly joyful as his health and spirits improved. He sent each completed song to Tonine via Sept-Epées, who relayed them with a smile, commenting, "See how our poor friend's attitude has changed! He thinks he is Béranger now! If you don't stop him, he will drown you in rhyme!"

"If he does, it will be the smartest thing he has done in his life," said Tonine after reading the songs. "Listen to them yourself, and tell me if you don't find them pleasing."

She sang for him in a fresh, pretty voice, without pretension, and Sept-Epées found the songs very much to his liking, which brought great pleasure to Tonine. Old Laguerre heard them as well. He hardly understood them, but he was determined not to disagree with any opinion voiced by his "princess" and pronounced them very nice indeed—though he assured himself privately that he could compose just as well if he so wished.

Tonine and Lise continued to sing Audebert's songs throughout town. One day, struck by a sudden inspiration, they induced Gaucher to deliver an envelope of the songs to the town's small newspaper, where they occasionally read the works of the town's amateur poets—none of them nearly as talented as Audebert, but published nonetheless. The following Saturday, the women were overjoyed to see the words to one of Audebert's songs in print. For the Black City's workers, this only served to confirm Audebert's talent, and Tonine fondly imagined that this new triumph would smooth the old man's way back into local society. Two or three young people with a talent for vocal music memorized the verses for a presentation with the town's choir. In the factory that employed Tonine, the voices of her fellow workers could soon be heard singing the song's stanzas. Audebert dissolved in tears of happiness, and was surrounded by well-wishers. He felt himself entirely welcomed by the town at last. There was a great deal of singing and very little work that day in the factory where Audebert now labored, but the next day, anxious to prove that poets are not necessarily lazy, Audebert set about his duties with a vengeance, and returned home that evening bursting with ideas for new verses and songs.

All the same, the old man did not greet his newfound glory without a few sighs of regret. For him, this small measure of success was but a glimmer of the brilliant achievements of which he had dreamed. Like many other members of the working class, Audebert had always harbored a certain prejudice against people with artistic tendencies. He had never viewed such pursuits as the work of a serious man.

Gaucher, who was a man of infallible good sense despite his simple nature, tried to shore up Audebert's confidence.

"Take heart, my friend. Popular songs seem to me to be very useful things. Take me—I am a simple man, as are many of us, and songs are a great boost to our morale, even when we do not realize it. Songs say a great deal in only a few words, and they reach even the most remote villages. They can soothe the spirit when one is sad, and they remind us of what is beautiful and good. I hope I won't offend you by saying this, but your other ideas—while they were admirable—might have been missing something here or there. There is certainly nothing lacking from your songs. You may not have been able to solve the world's problems, but it's a step in the right direction to make us forget those problems with song. If I were you, I'd be as proud of composing one lovely ballad as I would be if I had written a whole library's worth of books."

Audebert accepted Gaucher's words of wisdom gratefully, and he continued to report to work more or less regularly. He did not lack good intentions, but he found it difficult to sustain his good humor and he would weep like a child at the slightest hint of reproach. Lise, Tonine, and Gaucher made the old man an unofficial member of their family; he was almost like another child to them, in spite of the respect they had for his age and intelligence. They settled him in lodgings nearby, because they knew that his earning power had all but vanished, and that they could do little more than urge him to earn his daily bread when he felt up to it, raise his morale on the days when he succumbed to depression, and rein him in when his misplaced ambition began soaring too high. Tonine made sure that day-to-day life flowed as smoothly as possible for him by acting as a sort of liaison among his coworkers and his friends, and even the disjointed aspects of his own personality.

As for Sept-Epées, he worked as if the devil himself were at his heels, for he was determined to stabilize his finances so that Tonine would no longer have any excuse to refuse him. He was more in love with her than ever, and grew more and more impressed each day by her resilient spirits and graceful manners. She seemed suddenly beautiful, all the more so because of that certain air she possessed—a presence that set her apart from the other girls of the village. While they might imitate her hairstyle, her clothes, her walk, they could not duplicate the quality that made her a "princess," and though badly brought up young men continued to keep their distance from her, those with taste began flocking around her and competing with each other for the privilege of courting her.

Amidst this new flurry of attention, Tonine seemed to Sept-Epées to become a bit flirtatious, and he could not deny his jealousy. She did not exactly encourage any of her suitors, but rather she remained polite and high-spirited toward all of them. She did not try to conceal her fine figure or hide her natural radiance as she had in the past, when as a thin and gawky teenager she had been as skittish as a colt around everyone she met. She had finally been forced to admit that other people found her appealing, that they were drawn to her and wanted to please her, and that, at the moment, she was receiving attention from far too many suitors for her reputation to be endangered by the insolence of any single one of them. She walked in the Black City with her head held high; she spoke to everyone, freely gave and received advice, was careful never to find herself alone with any man. She was respectful of the elderly and respected by the young. She tried never to offend, and she found herself universally admired without ever having sought anyone's particular admiration.

Sept-Epées was proud of Tonine. He told himself that secretly she preferred him, but when he did not see evidence of this preference he tormented himself, and did not know what to make of the friendship she had offered him during more difficult times. He observed that she was generous and sensitive toward anyone around her who seemed to be suffering, and that she made it her duty to console those less fortunate than she. Her charitable qualities became more pronounced each day; after a restrictive and unhappy childhood she had become solicitous and nurturing, as if she had all of a sudden renounced her wish to live solely for herself.

Tonine had a delicate sense of propriety that won her respect everywhere she went. She continued to stay away from dances and other social events where young people were likely to quarrel among themselves. Working diligently in the paper factory, she reserved all of her leisure time for the contentment of her own good heart. If one of her acquaintances was ill, she unhesitatingly devoted to his care even the few moments she had to spare, and her presence alone had the effect of a soothing balm. She always found some item to give comfort to the poor, whether she took it from among her own store of possessions or solicited a charitable contribution from one of the town's wealthy citizens. If Laguerre fell into an unpleasant mood, she gently persuaded him to rise out of it. If Gaucher became momentarily downcast, Lise was quick to inform Tonine of it, and she would arrange a walk with the children to distract him.

Near her lodgings, Tonine kept a small plot of ground where she raised plants and flowers in stone pots. She took some new bit of flowering green to Audebert every Sunday, and reclaimed from him any previous week's offering that might require her care to regain its health. If a beau brought her flowers, she accepted them only with the proviso that they would be passed on to her dear "songwriter," to which the young men would smile and respond: "Very well, Tonine, if it pleases you."

Tonine's generosity to her friends was boundless. She had found the loveliest cat in the world for Laguerre, and she kept the animal as clean and white as ermine. She taught little Rose how to read and sew. She dressed her in pretty little frocks that she stitched with her own hands. She brushed the little girl's blond hair until it shone so brightly that Gaucher, coming home from the forge at night black with soot, thought he saw an angel waiting for him on the doorstep of their home. When the young men went hunting or fishing, she commandeered the game they brought home and cooked it for the town's invalids. The youths were only too happy to please her; indeed, they were known to squabble over who would have the honor of presenting her with a freshly caught rabbit or trout.

Sept-Epées watched everything, and smiled, and suffered,

but in truth he had no right to complain. If he went to her with the intention of airing his grievances, he invariably found her occupied in washing his clothes or preparing his supper as if she had become mistress and maid at the same time in the boarding house they shared—a role she acted in all of the homes that benefited from her tireless charity. Tonine managed to work unceasingly without coarsening her lovely white hands, which remained so smooth and beautiful that they were talked of even in the Upper Town, where they were the object of many women's envy.

Sept-Epées could not deny that Tonine was much beloved in their village, and he racked his brain to find ways to make himself more likable, more agreeable, and more special to her than all the others. He made sure to be in his godfather's room each night when Tonine came to look in on Laguerre, so that he might have a few moments to speak with her. Because the Lost Valley was a good distance away, he had no chance to see her during the day, while the other young workers who vied for her attention might easily encounter her at any moment of the day. Sept-Epées longed to go to her and ask to court her anew, but something in her attitude always prevented him from doing so.

Tonine kept a discreet distance from all who courted her. She maintained that no reasonable husband would allow her to give away money and goods as liberally as she wanted, and that if she married a man with the same habits as her own they would certainly end up in the poorhouse. Sept-Epées told himself that he had better amass a considerable fortune so that Tonine could always be as generous as she wished, and when jealousy caused him to slip a little in his work he redoubled his efforts, but without a great deal of success. His business contacts outside the town were not very reliable, and his deliveries were often late despite Va-sans-Peur's diligence.

Sept-Epées, in his more worried moments, imagined that Tonine could have brought him success, as had the genie for Aladdin, if she had loved him; but since she did not, he could not help but feel stiff and reserved around her. His pride did not easily tolerate the politeness and delicacy required to win a woman he had made wary of him through his own mistakes. Though generous and sincere, he did not know how to be tender. Proud of his work ethic and unfailing in his good conduct, he stood apart from most of his young contemporaries. He did not suffer injustice lightly. He viewed the lazy and the debauched with a sort of contempt, which, it must be owned, came largely from his godfather. The old man had brought up his young charge to abhor weakness, and when, as a child, Sept-Epées had asked forgiveness for some minor mistake, it was Laguerre's habit to say, in a voice like thunder, "None of that! Only babies beg for pity! Do not disobey me again—only thus will you earn my forgiveness."

Sept-Epées had inherited a good bit of his godfather's rigidity. He had hardly known the caresses of his mother, and he had never experienced the feeling of tender protectiveness toward a younger sister. His limitations were written on his handsome face, if one looked closely enough, and Tonine's gaze had perhaps penetrated the facade he showed the world, and she had been a bit frightened by what was revealed.

The young smith found himself feeling quite alone, and his bruised heart cried out in anguish, but he buried his feelings rather than admit to them. "What does it matter if I'm unhappy," he asked himself. "Unhappiness should not stop me from becoming a solid and worthy citizen! Indeed, all of this should make me stronger! Did Tonine not tell me that I must persevere in my efforts? Doubtless she would condemn me if I quit and came crying to her doorstep like a beaten dog. One day she will see me for who I really am, and my actions will speak a thousand times louder than any words I might utter."

Sept-Epées, unfortunately, had thus far failed to realize his dreams of success. He had neither strong mules to carry his merchandise, nor a good horse to carry him on his visits to outlying shopkeepers. He had to travel on foot, over lonely and often inhospitable terrain, and he lacked that persuasive quality so essential to a traveling merchant.

Business was not good. Sept-Epées had been wrong when he told himself that he understood the world of commerce. His upright and noble character rebelled against the thousand tiny tricks employed by the buyer and the seller; it mutinied against the disdain affected by those wishing to bring the price of a product down. Sept-Epées could not speak their language of jokes and lies and sometimes curses; it was completely at odds with his nature. He became angry when he was called a thief and a brigand, even though he knew that these were simply the pleasantries and banter of a transaction. It seemed that a man would kill for a discount of one or two francs.

One evening Sept-Epées returned to his factory disenchanted with his entire situation, and what he found there brought his frustration to the boiling point.

CHAPTER X

Va-sans-Peur was a man of impeccable honesty, and a worker devoted to his duty, but a bit excitable when the stresses of his job mounted too high. He had spent his entire adult life vigorously extolling the virtue and dignity of the laborer in the face of employers' unreasonable demands. Upon finding himself in a position of authority, however, he executed a rapid turnaround with the naiveté born of his lack of education and his tendency to live totally in a given moment. He spoke harshly to his old friends and demanded that his apprentices perfectly execute skills that they had not yet even learned. He refused to listen to any sort of criticism, and he swung all too easily between harsh reproach and outright threats in his dealings with the workers under him—the ultimate result of all this was that the factory was all but deserted on this particular day that Sept-Epées returned from one of his less than successful expeditions. Va-sans-Peur, when questioned, placed the blame on the absent workers, but to no avail; his young employer realized that his new overseer had irreparably damaged relations with nearly all of his employees.

For an instant, Sept-Epées remembered Audebert's passivity with nostalgia. The old man had treated the apprentices as if they were his children, and he had felt no qualms if he spent half an hour regaling the workers with the philosophies of Epicurus and Plato—regardless of the fact that he had never read any of their works. Va-sans-Peur, with the simple intention of running a tight ship, had caused nearly everyone to jump overboard.

Sept-Epées scoured the town, but could find no one willing to return to the factory under the direction of its intimidating new overseer. Obviously he had no choice but to dismiss Va-sans-Peur. Unfortunately, once that distasteful task had been accomplished, Sept-Epées found himself obligated to fill the position himself while he searched for a replacement. The majority of his employees were strangers to him, newly hired, and he had had precious little experience as a supervisor. After several days of struggling, he had also had enough. He resolved to close the factory and find another, better situated workshop, while losing as little money as possible in the process. When he tried to find another entrepreneur willing to purchase the Shack, however, the offers he received were so low as to discourage him terribly.

"Yes," he told himself, "Tonine was right. This location is worthless, and perhaps she realized that I am worthless as well."

The young man's unhappiness was increased by the prospect of returning to the manual labor he had once abjured as just a way to earn money, he who had been so proud of the quality of his handiwork. "She will loathe me for this," he told himself. "Once she admired my craftsmanship—she even called me an artist—but now, will she see any difference between me and the lowliest keymaker? If she were to see me now, how far I have fallen, unable even to make a living—no doubt she would double over with laughter at the idea of marrying me."

Shame overtook him. He decided that he could not bear to look Tonine in the eye until he had improved his situation. He came to a decision. As his godfather was well looked after at the Laurentis boarding house, there was no need for him to return to the Black City. He would not set foot there again until he had resolved the problem of his destiny. "I must improve myself for her sake," he told himself. "Since I'm obviously not suited to negotiate transactions, I must return to my old idea of finding a way to increase production speed and efficiency in our industries. It is rare to become rich off an invention, but it is at least honorable to create something new, and if I can improve the life of the common laborer, surely Tonine will be proud of me. And now, to work. Let the wind blow as it may. My little office will make a fine laboratory."

He rehired Va-sans-Peur to oversee his workers, but not without first admonishing him in carefully worded phrases about his conduct toward the employees and entreating him to keep matters calm at all costs. Then he installed himself in his small office in the upper gallery, and there he worked day and night, braving the cold when it began to creep into the building, and all the while designing, drawing, and constructing small models with heroic resolve.

Unfortunately, Sept-Epées's training matched neither his intelligence nor his desire. The scientific knowledge required for what he wished to accomplish lay beyond his capability. He began to encounter obstacles that he was unable to overcome. He searched his books for the answers he needed, but his library was small and he lacked the education to decipher what little information he was able to uncover. He did not dare venture into the Upper Town to consult the retired master workers who resided there; for he feared being taken for a fool, as Audebert had been, and he dreaded the possibility that gossip about his limitations would find its way to Tonine.

Time sped by, and Sept-Epées was forced to extend his research period to two months instead of the original one he had set aside. As the second month drew to a close and he found himself still no closer to revelation than he had ever been, despondency overwhelmed him. Having passed through various stages of hope, doubt, and disillusionment, he finally succumbed to fatigue. His efforts had shown him only that he knew nothing. He shivered against the bitter cold of winter in a bare and comfortless room, in the middle of a desolate wilderness, his head often aching, contemplating with a frozen heart the still faintly legible words that Audebert had scrawled on the wall, the night he had come so close to ending his own life. The barely discernible words would have made no sense to one who had never read them, but Sept-Epées knew them by heart, and sometimes he thought he could see them with a terrifying clarity, written not in coal but in blood.

The battle that he now fought for his pride proved a thousand times more arduous than the battles he had formerly fought for wealth. He no longer desired to become rich in order to win Tonine—he let his craving for wealth fall by the wayside and did not look back. His great object now was to convince himself of his own seriousness, his own worth. If he failed at this task, he knew he would succumb to despair.

Gaucher was concerned about him, and Tonine even more so. She questioned her cousin, who had gone several times to see the hermit in his cave in the Lost Valley, and had found him somber and silent. One day Tonine ventured out to the Shack with the Gauchers. On that particular occasion, Sept-Epées was feeling the effects of a vague sense of success, which rendered him a bit more hopeful, yet even less forthcoming. He was both touched and surprised by Tonine's visit, but when her reticence and dignity led her to leave the majority of the conversation to Lise his hope turned again to pain. He affected a nonchalant air and answered their questions about the state of his affairs with claims that everything was going well and he was content.

"But why do we never see you any more?" asked Tonine. "You are forgetting your godfather and your friends!"

"I haven't forgotten anyone, but you know, an owner's work is never done. Every time I leave this place, I find things in chaos when I return."

After several attempts to end the conversation, Sept-Epées finally agreed to spend *one* of his Sundays in the Black City, but when Lise invited him to supper the following

Sunday he avoided a definite commitment, saying only: "I will try, but don't wait for me."

"I'm afraid this may be the end of our friend," said Tonine to Lise as they returned to town.

"Why, do you think he is going to die?"

"I think that he is dead to friendship and that he lives now only to pursue his goals. Did you not see him, twenty-five years old, bent over his calculations as if he were a man of fifty?"

"Perhaps his business is not going well and he was ashamed to tell us," said Gaucher.

Tonine shook her head. "I thought we had shown him enough friendship in difficult times that he would not hide from us now as he did before. Haven't we done everything in our power to convince him that he can trust us? I don't like any sort of pride that leads a man to take his financial woes as much to heart as his romantic ones, and I must admit that I don't understand it at all. Where is the shame in failure if one has made a valiant effort? Where is the shame in being poor? Where does one acquire the notion that wealth is a duty? Does that mean that you and I, and the millions of hard-working people like us, who toil every day just to put bread on the table, are to be condemned and scoffed at?"

"What you do not see," responded Gaucher, "is that one's very soul can become a voice of torment, and that a man who honestly considers himself to be above those around him cannot be happy if he remains at the same level of success as they do."

"Ah," said Tonine. "Is that it? Well, then let us hope that

one day he will carry us upon his shoulders! By no means does he need our friendship! He has tried to convince us that he's happy, but after today I see that he cares about no one but himself."

"You seem full of spite, Tonine," observed Lise. "Why, when he came to you seeking your pardon, did you not forgive him?"

"Forgive him for what?" asked Gaucher, from whom his friend's conduct had been resolutely kept.

"For his ambition," replied Tonine. "You know the extent of his hunger always shocked me, and today it has shocked me even more, because I see that his ambition is consuming him, and that a tormented heart such as his will never be capable of building a happy life with another person."

Gaucher looked at his wife. "She's right," he admitted slowly. "Sept-Epées cannot remain a simple worker. I don't fault him for it; each man must pursue his own happiness in this vast world. But I am also filled with respect for the wishes of our dear cousin, who wants a husband all to herself, just as I am yours completely."

When the Gauchers and Tonine had returned to the Black City, Lise, finding herself alone with her cousin at the Laurentis rooming house, saw that the girl was struggling not to cry. Madame Laurentis noticed this too. She was a good woman, comfortably plump, with a sensitive understanding of matters of the heart, and she cherished Tonine almost as if she were her own daughter. She clucked disapprovingly in Lise's direction. "Do you know what is the matter? I do—she continues to lose sleep over that handsome young smith.

What is the matter with these 'worthy' young men—have they no feelings? Do they value anything other than money? If you care about our dear Tonine as much as I do, tell her to fix her heart upon someone else."

Tonine tried to hush Madame Laurentis, and quickly denied that she had any feelings of love for Sept-Epées—but, when pressed by the gentle questions of the two other women, she finally admitted that she had loved him once. Lise looked at her sympathetically. "And you love him still, do you not? Madame Laurentis tells me that you do not sleep well, and that sometimes you don't eat at all."

"It's all over now," insisted Tonine. "I have abandoned my foolish dreams and then taken them up again two or three times during the past year, but I've known all along that I would be unhappy with this young man—yes, unhappy in the worst way that a woman can be, for I know that I can't make him happy, either. If I'm crying now, it is because you have driven me to it by insisting that I'm in pain, and you are wrong about that. The easiest way to become sad is by complaining. Do you not see what I have accomplished by putting the welfare of others above my own? I have found consolation so great that I'm happy in spite of everything."

But Lise would not be deterred. "Perhaps," she persisted, "Sept-Epées suffers the same way that you do. If the two of you were to talk about this again, perhaps you would understand each other better."

Tonine shook her head. "No—we will not understand each other better, because we do not see things in the same way. If it's true that he suffers over me, then he is seeking his consolation in money, and that disgusts me, because the consolation that I have found is the antithesis of his."

"But, suppose he is trying to become rich so that he can do good, and so that he can give you the freedom to do good as well?"

Madame Laurentis rejoined the conversation. "Yes, have you considered that? I have known many young people who promise to give of their money freely as soon as they have earned it, but in the meantime they give in to temptation and waste the money on foolish pastimes. Heaven knows we are none of us saints—it's all too easy to give in to temptation. We cannot become rich overnight, my dear. These things take time. The only way to gain wealth is to stack one penny on top of another, and it takes a great deal of patience. We cannot rest until age and experience allow us to do so, and by then it is often too late to look with affection at the humble point we started from. We become hardened and cynical, all too aware of our faults and the faults of those around us. We learn the difficult lessons of distrust and fear. Come, my dear girls—I saw it happen to my poor husband, may he rest in peace, who began with one goat and ended with an entire hotel. He did not believe that he could succeed in this world by being soft, and he often beat the children and me, poor man! Woe to any girl who marries this Sept-Epées—whether he succeeds or fails, his wife will have to resign herself to the fact that each day he will sacrifice one more piece of his heart for the sake of another piece of gold in his purse. When a man has spent twenty or thirty years of his life arguing with his workers, always with the knowledge that his livelihood depends on their performance, is it possible that he will, one day, turn to his wife and say, 'Now, my dear, we have shared this long struggle, now let us share in its rewards'? No—God does not send us miracles such as that! And really, after so much time has passed it is not in any man's power to control his attitudes. He gradually becomes a miser. That is what I saw happen to my poor dear husband—he began so good, he ended so terrible! I wish I had been able to predict the future, to see what lay in store, the day he turned to me and said 'Let's build a hotel, and try to make it successful.' I should have stopped him—I should have said 'No, let's not build anything at all—let's keep our friends and our happiness instead!' "

This discourse by Madame Laurentis, delivered with the pleasure of a woman who enjoyed hearing herself speak but who said little that she did not have good reason to say, had a profound impact on Tonine; and Lise nodded her agreement as well.

"I see that you are full of good advice," she said. "Tonine is right to listen to you. Let's not speak any further of Sept-Epées. If he wishes us to forget him, let us forget him."

"No!" interjected Tonine. "He was my childhood friend, so I will always care about him whether my friendship matters to him or not, but I will torment myself no longer with his problems. As for marrying him, if he proposed to me again, I would not change the decision I made before."

Lise was convinced that any prospect of romance between her cousin and the young smith had been forever destroyed, and so she raised no objection in regard to a conversation she overheard several days later between her husband and Laguerre.

Gaucher had been approached by his employer, Monsieur Trottin, for whom Sept-Epées had also previously worked. Trottin had asked for news of the young man, and had added, "What the devil is that young man doing out there in the wilderness? He should sell that place before he loses it, and come back to work for us. Try to convince him, Gaucher. Tell him that I would be pleased to have him back, even though he left us so abruptly. That young man doesn't realize what he could earn in a workshop. If he had consulted me, I could have set him up with quite a comfortable situation—and who knows, I might still be able to find a good marriage for him!"

Laguerre's attention had been caught by this last statement, when Gaucher recounted his conversation with Trottin, who had a daughter named Clarisse. She was neither beautiful nor ugly—a bit simple-minded, perhaps, but she resided in a villa in the Upper Town and had no qualms about reminding others that her father ran a successful workshop in the Black City.

Trottin had fifty thousand francs invested outside his workshop. He had given ten thousand francs to each of his two older daughters, and Clarisse was to receive the rest. Trottin intended to retire to the Upper Town, and the prospect of a son-in-law such as Sept-Epées, who would be capable of taking over his business and ensuring that it continued to make a profit for the family, suited him nicely. This idea appealed greatly to Laguerre as well; the old man believed he had finally hit upon a way to be sure that his dear godson would be more comfortable financially than he himself had been, and also to keep him in the Lower Town more or less permanently. He assigned Gaucher the task of broaching the marriage scheme to Sept-Epées.

Sept-Epées was at the height of his efforts and hopes when this bombshell was dropped upon him. He resisted committing himself one way or the other, and spoke vaguely of Tonine. Gaucher, who wished ardently for his friend's happiness and still believed him capable of realizing his ambitions, tried to steer his thoughts away from Tonine by reminding him that she was determined not to marry. Finally, Sept-Epées hung his head in defeat and allowed Gaucher to extol the virtues of Mademoiselle Trottin without really listening to him, but also without protesting. Finally, he agreed to return to the Trottin workshop, but he made no commitment beyond that. He told himself that if he did not wish to sink further into debt and permanently establish a reputation as a failure, he must grit his teeth and attach himself to the ball and chain once more.

CHAPTER XI

When Tonine heard that Sept-Epées had not said no, and that Gaucher had begun to investigate venues for the proposed wedding, she was overcome by a new wave of sadness and wept in secret. She tried to hide her grief from everyone, especially Madame Laurentis, and maintained a mask of gaiety that she never allowed to fall for even an instant.

The day after the conversation between Gaucher and Sept-Epées, Tonine went to visit her friend Rosalie Sauvière, who had broken her arm. On her way, she encountered young Doctor Anthime, who had cared for Audebert at the Shack. Their paths had crossed several times before, in similar circumstances, but she had seen in his eyes that he fancied her and had taken care to keep her distance from him. Today, however, downcast and a bit distracted, she did not particularly notice that the doctor lingered at her friend's house longer than was necessary—and anyway, it seemed impossible that he would dare to make advances to her in the presence of Rosalie and her mother. So it was a great shock to her when he took her hand, saying, "Mademoiselle

Tonine, I have something very important to tell you, something I've been wanting to say for quite some time. I am even glad for the presence of Madame Sauvière and her daughter, because they shall bear witness to my good intentions. I have been in love with you since the first time we met, and there has been so much talk lately of your goodness and generosity in town that I have obtained my father's permission to ask for your hand in marriage. My father, as you know, is something of a philosopher, and he is delighted when the heart and the mind are in agreement. He asked to hear all about you, and he supports my decision. We aren't a wealthy family, but I am the only son, and I have already developed a roster of loyal clients. I'm a good and honest man, Tonine. Will you take some time to think over my proposal? If there is anything you wish to know about me, please ask. Give me your answer soon—I won't rest until I know your decision."

Tonine was so stunned by Anthime's words, and by the simple and sincere manner in which he had spoken them, that she found herself at a loss as to what to say.

"Doctor Anthime has spoken to you in all seriousness, my dear," said Madame Sauvière gently. "He does you a great honor by asking for your hand in marriage, and I hope you will not reflect long before you give him your answer."

"No," replied Tonine, "I will not reflect very long at all. I may say right now that I'm grateful to Doctor Anthime, and that I hold him in great esteem for loving a girl with no dowry other than her good reputation, but I really do not wish to marry, and even if I did wish it a little, I would only do so with the understanding that I wouldn't be forced to leave my home, where I have many old friends, for I think of the honest people here as my family."

"It's true that you are beloved by many families here," said Madame Sauvière. "You are wise to want to marry her, Doctor Anthime, for she is the epitome of honor and it would please us all to see her comfortably settled. However, each of us must pursue her own happiness above all else, and I will say nothing to prevent Tonine from rising up through the ranks of society. She will be able to win the affection of whatever circle of people she joins."

"I care nothing for rank," broke in Tonine. "On the contrary—I despise the very notion of it."

"A doctor's rank, if you may call it that, seems very well suited to your desire to help the poor," said Anthime.

"You're right," admitted Tonine, "but I cannot see myself leaving the Lower Town. I have found too much affection here to be content with what little friendship I might find elsewhere. In marrying you, I would be forced to become a society wife in the Upper Town, and I would be ridiculed as my poor sister was. Do you not see that I have nothing but painful memories of that place? I will never again live there by choice."

"But that means nothing!" burst out Anthime. "If you wish to stay here, then I will move, for I would certainly be of more use here, where you have only one doctor among you, than in the Upper Town, where I have several competitors! You will not have to change a single one of your habits, Tonine, and you will have done your fellow citizens a service besides."

This response made an impression on Tonine, and she asked for eight days in which to make her decision.

"I don't ask that you keep my proposal a secret," said Anthime as he was leaving. "On the contrary—I hope you will ask the advice of your closest friends. Whatever your decision, Tonine, I will never regret having fallen in love with a girl such as you."

Tonine was so flattered by Anthime's conduct that she did not refuse him a handshake, and she also allowed Madame Sauvière and Rosalie to congratulate her as if she were already engaged. Indeed, she was still a bit intoxicated by the morning's events when she returned home that afternoon, and she could not resist running to tell Lise what had happened. Lise, enchanted, rushed to deliver the news to Gaucher, who was overjoyed. "If it was any other bourgeois," he said, "I would sooner break his neck than give my consent. I learned my lesson all too well from what happened to your poor sister. But Doctor Anthime—that's different! He is the son of the bravest and best man in the world, and he himself has a fine and generous heart, just like his father. I have seen him tending to sick people—he does not just care for them, he loves them. Yes, yes, Tonine, he is surely the man for you, and it seems to me that God has sent him to you as compensation for the pain that Molino brought to our entire family."

Tonine passed the rest of the afternoon seeking the advice of Madame Laurentis, Father Laguerre, and Audebert, all of whom agreed with Gaucher. Laguerre was a bit distrustful of doctors, but when he learned that it was

Anthime's habit to treat the Black City's citizens for free, he grudgingly admitted that here was a doctor worth admiring.

For his part, Sept-Epées, upon hearing the news, could not help but recall the offer of a financially advantageous marriage that he himself had lately received. The thought of acquiring a fortune so easily was certainly tempting, especially to a young man whose heart had been so bruised by his only experience with love. If Gaucher had only come to him with Trottin's offer a few months earlier, the young smith mused, he would have had no qualms about accepting, but his admiration for Tonine had lately turned to passion, and her image haunted him with such persistence that he resolved to go and find her, to tell her of his feelings, and to vow to her that he would sacrifice everything else if she would only consent to be his wife.

That evening, Sept-Epées returned to the Black City late—he had been detained by some business in the Upper Town, and it was nearly ten o'clock. Not wishing to wake his godfather, who was long asleep by this hour, he entered the house without making a sound. He had seen a light burning in Tonine's window; it was her habit to sit up sewing long into the night. He started up the stairs to her room; he was intending to knock on the door and ask to speak with her the next morning, since he knew she would never allow him into her room so late at night.

The staircase to the upper floor of the rooming house was an exterior one, cut into the rock of the cliff upon which the building perched. To reach Tonine's apartment, it was necessary to cross the small terrace where she had set out her flowerpots. Sept-Epées was picking his way carefully across the stones, so as not to stumble in the darkness, but was brought up short when he heard Lise's voice, in Tonine's chamber, mention his name. Straining to make out what was being said, he sat down quietly on the doorstep. He promised himself that he would confess to this indiscretion in the morning, but he was unable now to resist the desire to listen. The door was rather thin, and he heard everything.

Tonine had apparently wished to know what Sept-Epées's intentions were regarding Mademoiselle Trottin, and when Lise had pressed Laguerre for information, in his excitement at the idea of seeing his godson comfortably established in the Lower Town, he had implied incorrectly that the Trottin matter was all but settled. As a result, at the very moment that Sept-Epées mounted the stairs to Tonine's room to tell her that he loved and desired only her, Lise was saying that the girl should feel free to do whatever she wished where Anthime was concerned.

Like any woman, Tonine could not help but be flattered and a bit excited at the prospect of the future she had been offered. She was proud that she might be the means of bringing another skilled doctor to the Lower Town. In her head, she had already begun to plan new charitable projects, and she and Lise delighted in discussing the simplicity and elegance with which she might decorate a new home. Tonine had long dreamed of a bright little cottage on the banks of a clear stream just south of the Black City, with a view of the trees and a little garden where her poor rosebushes, now languishing in their stone pots, might flourish in sunlight and open air. Childlike despite her wisdom, Tonine asked Lise if she had ever dreamed of an arbor of camellias in pink and white, like the one that had been in the garden of her former brother-in-law when her sister Suzanne had presided over the Molino household.

"My poor sister," Tonine mused, "she found precious little happiness when she changed her station in life! She was content with her jewels and pretty clothes, though, and so determined to give me airs and—despite my wishes—make me wear a bonnet! Do you think, Lise, that my husband will want me to wear a bonnet? That would bother me greatly, and I would certainly never wish to resemble Clarisse Trottin, who looks like a beet in a basket!"

Tonine broke into laughter—determined as she was never to wear a bonnet, she was also secretly pleased by the idea that she would be entitled to wear one if she chose. Suddenly she stopped laughing, and her face became serious. "We are talking of the external pleasures of marriage, but one must start with a solid foundation, and I cannot have that if I don't love my husband!"

"You will grow to love him," said Lise soothingly.

"I will try my best, for he certainly deserves my respect and affection. All the same—"

"All the same, what? He isn't a bad fellow; his manners are lovely, and he is young and elegant. And I have a feeling, my dear, that once he loves it is for a lifetime! When you find yourself loved so completely, it will be impossible for you not to love him back with your whole heart."

"Do you really believe that, Lise? I hope it will be as you predict! For the moment, the idea of loving a man whom I hardly know seems quite silly! And that is not all. I have this heaviness pressing on my heart, and I don't know what it is."

Lise looked concerned. "Are you still thinking of Sept-Epées?"

"No—of course not—but I don't want my happiness to cause pain to anyone else. I would like to be sure that he wants to marry Clarisse Trottin."

"You are really too selfless. Sept-Epées is going to be rich, which should console him for almost anything else."

"But if his greatest worry is having disappointed me, nothing can help him. Ah, well, God willing, I will be married soon and Sept-Epées will regret nothing! Perhaps I will even be happy, who knows?"

Lise nodded. "Yes—you have spent enough time thinking of others' happiness. It's time for you to think of yourself a little!" She kissed Tonine and left without seeing Sept-Epées, who hid in the shadows as she passed by.

He remained where he was for nearly an hour, grappling with the idea of knocking on Tonine's door and crying, "Do not marry Anthime, Tonine—I will die if you do!" But his masculine pride would not allow him to do it, and he fled into the mountains to escape temptation, and to think.

Alone in the woods, he gave in to grief and disappointment as he wandered aimlessly until daybreak. When the sun began to rise, he calmed himself and gathered his thoughts. He knew that Tonine had every right to settle into marriage with someone other than him, and her words to

Lise the night before had convinced him that vengeance was the last thing on her mind; indeed, she had tormented herself with the idea that by marrying another she might be harming him. Nowhere was her generous soul so evident than when she showed herself willing to give up everything she stood to gain by marrying Anthime, in order to avoid hurting a friend who had himself been inexcusably selfish with regard to her. He knew that it would take only a word from him to induce Tonine to reject Anthime forever, and thus to sacrifice the charitable pursuits and the peaceful riverside cottage of which she had always dreamed. Sept-Epées saw everything clearly—Tonine did not love him with any sort of passion, and she did not want to be his wife, but she treasured their longtime friendship to such an extent that she could not be happy unless he was happy as well.

With this conviction fixed in his mind, Sept-Epées believed he understood what he must do. "She must not see me suffer," he told himself. "She must not miss this chance for happiness. She has found a young man who loves her as she deserves to be loved, and better, apparently, than I knew how to love her. I must not stand in the way of her marriage—it is the only way I can make up for my shameful behavior toward her. She must not see my jealousy or my pain. I have conquered love once with my ambition—now I must conquer it again, this time with my honor."

When Sept-Epées returned to the Shack, where he found Va-sans-Peur already at work, his pallor startled the other man, who had a sensitive and affectionate nature that was belied by his rough exterior. Sept-Epées, seeing tears of shock and worry welling in Va-sans-Peur's eyes, could not hold his own emotions in check any longer. He cried with abandon, and felt a good deal better afterward.

He collapsed onto his cot and slept for several hours, calmer now that he had realized the extent of his misery and had resolved to conduct himself nobly in the midst of it. Around noon, he rose, spent some time putting his accounts in order, filled his pockets with about half of what little money he had, and gave the other half to Va-sans-Peur, saying, "I know that you are a true friend, and I'm grateful to you for that. Don't worry about me—I'm brave enough, and a bit of traveling will be good for me. I will be gone for some time. I'm leaving you in charge of the workshop and all my possessions, and you are to receive half of the factory's profits while I'm gone. If you prefer to close the Shack and return to work in town, that is certainly your right. I know you will do what is best, but there's one thing I ask of you, as a friend and on your word as an honest man—that is that you do not worry anyone on my account. You must promise me this as solemnly as if I had only an hour left to live."

When Va-sans-Peur had given his word, Sept-Epées added, "Please do not trouble yourself about me. I, too, give you my word as an honest man that I will do no harm to myself."

He signed a piece of paper confirming Va-sans-Peur's right to run the factory and receive half of its profits in his absence, and asked that nothing be said of his departure until after he had written to his friends himself. He shook Va-sans-

Peur's hand, took the midday meal and a glass of wine with him, and then, slinging his rucksack and tools over his shoulder, he climbed the ravine wall and started down the road to Lyon.

No one discovered that day or the next that he was gone. It was only on the third day that Laguerre received a letter from him, sent from Saint-Etienne, in which Sept-Epées sounded happy enough, and wrote that he wished to see the factories at Forez to learn about certain manufacturing procedures he might be able to use at home. Another day he wrote to Gaucher, and finally, on yet another, to Tonine herself.

"My dear neighbor," he wrote, "allow me to write to you with my best wishes and a heartfelt request that you look after my dear godfather, to whom you have always been so kind. I am obliged to leave town for a while, wishing to devote myself entirely to business, which I would never have been able to do without your kindness in taking such an interest in Father Laguerre's comfort. I am extremely grateful for everything you have done for him and for me as well, and I wish you to know that I have no ill will toward you or anyone else. I hope you will think of me kindly as well, and I give you my very best regards.

"Your servant and friend, Etienne Lavoute, Sept-Epées."

Tonine was convinced that anyone who could have written such a letter must possess a tranquil heart and a head full of positive ideas. She rejoiced with Lise, yet was unable to feel truly joyous at the bottom of her heart. Two days later, she had begun to make plans and allow herself to be congratulated on her forthcoming marriage by a crowd of friends. Her numerous beaux were not in the least pleased, but since she had never encouraged any of them too strongly, they did not have much cause for complaint. No one could say that Tonine lacked modesty even as she accepted congratulations, and her happiness at not having to leave the Black City was evident to everyone.

The eighth day approached quickly, the day on which she had promised to give Doctor Anthime her answer to his proposal of marriage. She had given him permission to come to her at the Gaucher home at two o'clock in the afternoon. The night before they were to see each other, however, she was seized by a sudden wave of panic, and all her dreams of comfort and security seemed worthless. In forcing herself to think of everything she could gain by marrying Anthime, she had stifled her dreams of true companionship and happiness.

"Don't speak to me any more of the house on the riverbank, or of the garden of camellias," she said to Lise. "I am accustomed to not having pretty things, and in truth I don't really need them. I would doubtless tire of my gilded cage all too quickly—I think I have begun to do so already. I want to be consumed with excitement at the thought of my marriage, of coming to love this man I hardly know, but I cannot, Lise—I don't feel anything for him, and I must make an effort even to remember all of his good qualities. If this were to continue, do you not see that I would be the unhappiest of women, and I would do better to throw myself into the ravine?"

Tonine barely slept that night, and when she did she dreamed of Sept-Epées, sad and ill, even dead, and she woke so paralyzed with fear at this nightmare that she got out of bed, lit her lamp, and read again the letter that he had written to her. The words seemed calm, even content, but upon closer inspection it could be seen that tears had fallen onto the paper, and the address had been written in a shaky hand. The whole truth rushed in on her with overwhelming force, and as soon as the sun began to rise she hastened to the Shack.

She plied Va-sans-Peur with questions. In spite of his promises of discretion he could not resist her obvious distress, and he told her that Sept-Epées had left town like a man at the end of his rope, on the brink of succumbing to despair. Tonine asked permission to go into the factory's little office and write a letter to Sept-Epées.

"My dear friend," she wrote, "in response to your kind letter I must tell you that your godfather is doing very well, and that I am taking very good care of him. I am doing this out of the great friendship that I have for you as well as for him, because you are two of the most important people in my life. I hope that your business goes well and that it makes you happy. For my part, I am content to remain as I am, for, as you know, I am not inclined to marry. I have time now to think about it, however, as do you. While I wait for your return, I will remain your devoted friend and companion for life,

"Jeanne-Antoinette Gaucher."

She sealed the letter, wrote Sept-Epées's last known

address on the envelope, and returned to town, where she hurried to the post office. Feeling a great deal more at ease after having mailed the letter, she awaited her interview with Anthime.

CHAPTER XII

Sept-Epées did not receive Tonine's letter. He was no longer staying in the town from which he had written to his friends by the time their replies arrived. He traveled without any clear idea of his destination; he knew only that he wished to get as far away from the Black City as he could, and to forget his sorrows for a little while. He did not really expect to receive any response to his letters, anyway—and he believed that the best thing he could do was to try to block out all thoughts of what might be going on back home.

He knew that his small store of money would not last very long, and he planned to try to find work at the next factory he came upon so that he could earn the funds he needed to continue his voluntary exile. He stopped in the first town he arrived at and worked there for a few weeks; then, curious to try his luck in an arena grander than what he'd been accustomed to, and perhaps to gain new skills as well, he set off for a larger city.

After several months of traveling and learning in this random manner, Sept-Epées chanced to receive a letter from

Gaucher, who wrote positively of Laguerre's health and the slow but satisfactory progress of the Shack under Va-sans-Peur's direction. Sept-Epées realized that his overseer was considerably more knowledgeable about figures than he himself, and he affirmed a thought that had been lingering in his mind since the beginning of his travels: a small business cannot prosper without unfailing tenacity, resignation to difficulty, and an often shocking measure of stinginess. It is all too easy for a man to dream of rapid progress without admitting to himself the difficulty of generating anything in abundance when one begins with but little, and the disillusionment that accompanies the realization of this simple if harsh fact can prove fatal to even the most ardent visions of success. Consumed by worry, hoping for the best but constantly being hindered by lack of money, Sept-Epées had been unable to satisfy himself with tiny gains. But Va-sans-Peur, resolute and obstinate, worked each day with the diligence of a team of oxen, and he never stopped to fret about tomorrow. Although his inability to read made it impossible for him to keep any written records, he was able to memorize every detail of daily business with the miraculous exactitude of a mind able to rely totally on itself. No torments of imagination or self-esteem distracted him from his task. In short, in his hands the Shack began to produce a small but secure profit. Hoping to double his initial investment in just a few years, Sept-Epées in his pride had expected wondrous success to occur easily, but such wonders more often come only from exceptionally hard work.

Witnessing the drama of daily human life and availing

himself of any opportunity to work that he came across in his travels, the young smith became more and more aware of the ways of the world, and convinced himself that he was not being unwise to save his money—but he would certainly never have enough to buy a painted house with a flowering garden in the Upper Town. This was by no means a disappointment to him, and by itself would not have bothered him a bit, but for the regret he associated with it of not marrying Tonine. He thought with bitterness of the happiness that had come to Gaucher, who, living solely for the objects of his loving affection, had so easily forgotten the temptations of an independent life. Such austere happiness, which had seemed to Sept-Epées like a torture of humiliation and confinement, now seemed to him to be like a vanishing mirage in the desert of his misery. In his letter, Gaucher did not mention Tonine's name. She, having received no response from Sept-Epées, had convinced herself that she had been foolish in her tenderness for him. Sept-Epées continued to write to his other friends from time to time, his brief notes always affecting happiness and tranquility, and he never asked about Tonine. He believed her to be married, and he did not want to know anything further about it. Gaucher's silence on this point only served to reinforce his conclusion. Gaucher also wrote that Sept-Epées should have received letters from others in town. "Hm—I have received nothing," thought the young man to himself, "and all the better for me! Doubtless the others wrote to me about the wedding and Doctor Anthime's welcome presence in town. I have nothing to do with any of that now. I did my best to avoid standing in the way of their happiness, and there is no need for me to hear the particulars of it."

Everywhere Sept-Epées broke his journey, he was recognized as a first-rate worker and his services were much in demand. He had no specialty; that is to say, he was not one of those workers who spend their entire careers perfecting one skill without ever learning another. In a large workshop, manufacturing resembles a song, with each man assigned to a particular note that he produces without paying attention to any that come before or after it. A worker of expert caliber, however, is able to move from one task to another with as much ease as if he has been trained in each skill since childhood. Sept-Epées was such a worker, and whether he set himself to the production of fine-bladed knives or glittering firearms, the end product was invariably exquisite. He had an innate love of beautiful things. When he had the opportunity to study the creation of delicate scissors or elegant masks, he seized it with pleasure. His craft was very nearly an art already, and in his capable and tasteful hands it became one.

"But what good does it do me to learn all of this?" he asked himself in his moments of sadness or reflection. "I will never have the opportunity to make anything but crude tools in the Black City, for originality and inspiration have no place there. And whenever I leave one place and establish myself in another, how can I escape the idea that there must always be something better somewhere else? How will I ever be satisfied?"

He studied mechanics as well, and at first felt humbled when he saw a thousand projects and inventions, of which he had only dreamed, applied in ways more perfect than he had ever imagined. Everywhere he went, it was the same story—ideas, methods, and innovations that would not work in the Black City for a variety of reasons: lack of means, lack of space, lack of powerful enough motors or forceful enough waterfalls, lack of manpower, lack of capital. It was easy enough to see what was needed back home, but implementing such improvements was a different matter altogether—and scientific achievement depends on a balance between ideas and means. Occasionally, the power of genius may be great enough to overcome a lack of readily available resources, but, far more often, misplaced ambition combined with unfocused effort leads to failure and stagnation.

Sept-Epées found some consolation in observing the rapid diffusion of innovative inventions and the ease with which they were absorbed and perfected by intelligent local practitioners. The young man gradually moved beyond the shallow illusions of fame and fortune that he had cherished in earlier days; he became calmer, more objective, and wiser as he observed in the different workshops many capable men who improved upon the procedures they performed each day without losing themselves to arrogance. He recognized that great inventors were becoming more and more rare, and that one day it might even be impossible to discern who was responsible for each new innovation.

All of these reflections, combined with the conversations that Sept-Epées had with the educated business owners and talented workers in each town, gave the young man a more balanced outlook and a modest quality that he had previously lacked. He gave up the scorn he had always had for small projects, and realized that one need not feel ashamed if he is not called to some exalted destiny. Audebert, he realized, was a perfect example of what havoc the industrial age had wreaked, and he himself had been all too close to following the same destructive path. Only his youth and clear head had spared him.

His painful experience with love had also taught him a difficult, but useful, lesson. A mistake may often be of ultimate benefit to the soul, as long as the mistake is reparable and the soul is generous. If the young man had truly hurt Tonine, he had also regretted it for a very long time, and he had earned the right to a clear conscience.

Eventually, his travels took him as far as the French border and then across it into Germany. All the while he moved restlessly from one place to another, he insisted to himself that an active and serious life would prove to be the cure-all for his unhappiness. He felt himself to be master of his own fate, but only when he was on the move. As soon as he began to develop any sort of friendship in one town or another, the glimpse of domestic felicity it provided overwhelmed him with the recognition of his own heart's emptiness, and there was certainly no shortage of friendly encounters. His talent and gentlemanly manners disposed people to welcome him wherever he went, and his small business, of which Gaucher's letters provided proof, put him in an elite class of artisans. However, the moment he responded to the friendly overtures of the local families, he found himself so overcome by emotion that he was obliged to flee. The image of Tonine appeared between him and every new sight that met his eyes. It was as if she had cast a spell over him, and indeed, after a fashion, so she had.

Sept-Epées encountered many beauties in Germany, buxom girls with golden hair, turquoise eyes, rosy cheeks, innocent faces, and vacant smiles. They seemed to beckon to his starving soul with promises of tranquility and security. If he was momentarily touched by their sentimental and trusting natures and by the fact that they seemed to want nothing more than to cherish and care for him, he quickly told himself that he was no more special to these girls than any other man: they desired someone, anyone, to love—his particular identity was of little consequence. He did not wish to fulfill anyone's fantasy. Any other young man could do that as well as he. Always he dreamed of the princess of the Black City, with her pale loveliness, her mysterious air, her quiet gaiety and unaffected generosity, her sensitivity and magnanimity. Tonine was a woman unlike all others, and with every thought of her Sept-Epées felt that he rose above his station, just as with thoughts of anyone else he sank beneath it.

Sept-Epées was also a victim to that law of human nature which states that unrequited love clings to one more tenaciously than any other sort. It is a sad truth that one remembers the lover who rejected him far longer than the one who brought him a measure of happiness. Sept-Epées struggled bravely with his pride, the dangers of which he had recognized long ago, but one can never change completely, and he carried within his heart a wound that refused to heal.

His disappointment returned with a start whenever he was on the brink of forgetting, and it was at these moments that he again pushed forward on his restless journey, while telling himself: "I must have more time. My pain will pass eventually, perhaps when I least expect it."

One day, in response to a reproving letter from Gaucher, he broke forth with an account of everything he had suffered, everything he had felt, everything he had examined and changed within his own soul. He refrained from mentioning Tonine, but his secret was easily guessed. His letter was sincere, dignified, and touching in its tone and content. He closed it by saying, "You must forgive me, my faithful friend, for having waited so long to open my heart. I have been awaiting a moment of calm which has not yet come but which seems closer now than it did in the past. There have been days when I was almost content with this life of searching for answers that I do not seem to be able to find on my own. There is one thing that would, perhaps, give me a little peace, and that is to know if the person to whom I have devoted so many of my thoughts is as happy in her marriage as she deserves to be. I know I have not asked about her until now, and if I do not do so again, it will not be because I have forgotten her—on the contrary—but I hope that the time may come when I can hear her spoken of without feeling the urge to weep.

"I am writing to you from a very beautiful country, where I plan to remain for some time and where your letters will easily find me. I can even tell you that, for perhaps the tenth time, I have some hope of marrying here, but I cannot tell if my chances are better here than they have been anywhere else. My heart does not seem able to rouse itself. No matter—my consolation shall be that your heart pulses with warmth, and so does that of Lise, and so do those of your children, who are doubtless strong and beautiful these days. I am honored to hear that you have given your new baby my name—it is proof that you have not forgotten me. I hope that little Etienne will never suffer as I have done, and that he will in time become a happy man. If I ever have the pleasure of seeing him, I will tell him that the greatest happiness in life comes from love and friendship, and that nothing else we seek so arduously in this wide world is worth the effort of chasing it."

The country estate on which Sept-Epées found himself was owned by a wealthy widow, three or four years older than the young smith, but quite agreeable and possessing a pale brunette beauty that reminded him somewhat of Tonine's. This time he made a sincere effort at a romantic attachment, not out of any real attraction to the widow—her appeal lay in the memories she stirred of another—but because of the pleasure he took in the beautiful countryside, and in his hopes for a life of peace and productivity.

He had encountered the widow purely by chance. She had taken an immediate fancy to him, and had contrived to detain him by asking his advice regarding the repair of an agricultural machine, and he had then amused himself by tinkering with it. He had been with her for a little more than a month now, but he'd said nothing about a permanent commitment, as he knew full well that she was eager to devote herself to him completely. She spoke French fairly well, and Sept-Epées had learned a bit of German. Seated one day beneath a magnificent willow tree, he watched the widow as she read poetry on the veranda of her substantial farmhouse. She was certainly not ugly when viewed at close range, and, seen from afar, her slender waist and graceful bearing gave her a distinct beauty. The plump cows and woolly sheep on the grounds surrounding her, the white house fenced by flowering hedges, the varicolored trees and green hills blending into a verdant sea, and the delicately tinted sky combined to form a serene and harmonious tableau.

The gentle spring breeze rustled softly in the pines and carried their fresh scent to the young man's nose. "Here is happiness," he thought to himself, "if not for me, then for someone with the wisdom and patience to truly appreciate it. An active heart would certainly grow restless and stifled under so placid a routine. Nature reigns supreme here; time flows in measured beats, hour by hour, day by day, and it obeys no man's will. A place such as this scoffs at our fevered bursts of activity. But it is also a sort of trap; once one has wedded himself to this earth, it is impossible to leave it. Here is a workshop that does not move, that must be protected not only from other men but also from the birds in the sky and the insects hiding in the grass. It is a net woven of flowers, a soft and sensuous cage.

"And yet, I cannot deny the grandeur of the countryside! The artisan's most ingenious productions pale in comparison with the majesty of an ancient wood! How vast the sky is, arching smoothly and endlessly over these perfect fields!

And there is no music sweeter than the rustling of the leaves as the breeze caresses them. Here, one finds no place for all-consuming pride, or for the woes of the tortured soul—here, one must fight against the powerful charms of this illusion of peace, which hides the mysterious and unceasing labors of the earth.

"Yes, here one must better himself, or at least embrace greater dignity and austerity. Vanity, sensitivity, ambition, all must yield to a sort of healthy fatalism. The steel and fire of an industrial life is a sort of delirium, an unending battle with nature and one's own self. The life of a country peasant is a sort of prolonged submission, half prayer and half slumber. The peasant's disdain for the torments and joys that consume us in industry is written on his face, he who neither laughs nor cries. He contemplates, and he meditates. He is constantly awaiting something that he knows, little by little, sooner or later, will eventually come. Whereas the artisan, buried in the mines or closed in a dark workshop, is forever fixing his eyes and his spirit upon a single narrow focus, the farmer looks only to the wide expanse of sky, from which the rays of sun and drops of rain will surely descend to put the finishing touches on his masterpiece. Both the laborer and the farmer produce and create by the sweat of their brows; but while the artisan fashions something that will exist only as long as it is useful and then disappear, something transitory and fragile whose destiny its creator can never know, the farmer nourishes something eternal, a thing that may slumber but will then live again under his hands, something active and inexhaustible that will flower each year, and bear fruit beneath his very gaze."

These were the young man's thoughts, which occurred in vivid images rather than words. He thought little of the widow, but he felt himself falling in love with the countryside. He recalled the earliest years of his childhood in the barren, rocky valley where he had been born and where he had been a barefoot and ignorant boy, unaware that anything better might exist for him. "And why did I not remain that way?" he asked himself. "I would certainly not have suffered as much as I have. Everything I have gained has only made me more aware of what I do not have. Now, if I could forget what is in my past and be content to work without passion, to marry without love, to live in ignorance of the future, I could finally have peace amidst these green hills and this pure sky. I could live like a child again—the squeal of a newborn goat, the cluck of a chicken outside my window, the thump of my boots on newly plowed earth, these would be the simple joys of my life. Who knows—I might even be truly content one day, and burst with pride at the cattle fattening in my stables!"

Sept-Epées was roused from his daydreams by the hurried footsteps of a boy bearing a letter. He had evidently run from one farm to another for some time seeking the man whose name was hastily scrawled on the envelope. It was from the Black City, and though the stamp on it was several weeks old, Sept-Epées saw the following message written beneath the address:

"Extremely urgent—deliver immediately."

CHAPTER XIII

The letter was from Lise Gaucher. In her haste she had written the address incorrectly.

"My dear friend," she wrote, "unless your heart has completely changed, it is time for you to return home. Your godfather is well, as are Louis and I, but poor Tonine has been ill for some time. She cannot work, and she finds herself in so much debt from her medical costs that it would take a miracle to set her affairs to rights again. Without our friendship and devotion to her, I believe she would be done for. She is so upset at the idea that we are sacrificing ourselves by helping her, however, that we fear she will die rather than continue viewing herself as a burden. She is quite in torment. Our thoughts have often turned to you; you are fairly well off and have no family to support. Perhaps if you were to come home, you could persuade Tonine to accept the help of an old friend that she certainly deserves."

So Tonine was not married! Joy was the first feeling that rushed over Sept-Epées, but it was quickly replaced by worry. Tonine was ill, only her condition could not be hopeless; otherwise, they would not have called upon him to help her. Love can work miracles, and Sept-Epées realized at that moment that he was as much in love with Tonine as ever.

His vague dreams of pastoral happiness vanished in an instant. He looked around as if he was awakening from a deep sleep. The rolling plains seemed suddenly flat and empty, the white farmhouse pretentious, the animals dirty and malodorous, and the widow without youth or charm. When he brushed past her to gather his things, she clung to his arm and asked anxiously if he meant to leave her. "Yes!" he replied brusquely. "Did I promise you I would stay? My wife is ill! Farewell! It was my pleasure to work for you. Keep your money, I do not want it." And, feeling as light as a bird soaring on the spring breeze, he fled. He hailed the first coach he saw, then caught a train, and in less than five days he found himself standing at the head of the mountain road that wound down the steep cliffs to the noise and smoke of the Black City.

It was nearly a league's distance from the top of the gorge to the ravine floor. He walked so quickly that his footsteps left barely a trace on the sandy road, and his heart thumped in his chest. How noble and beautiful everything looked, here in his dear Trou d'Enfer! The green fields and orchards of the German widow seemed far away, like something in a dream. Here, he reveled in the rocky cliffs, in the dark, windswept woods, in the narrow passages lit by errant sunbeams and overflowing with wild greenery. Love and hope seemed to radiate from the abundance of nature surrounding him.

He came to a point that he knew lay just above his factory. There was no time to climb down to it now; he was anxious to reach his friends as soon as possible. He intended to continue his journey along the lower road, which stretched parallel to the river and would get him home quickly, but he could not resist stopping for this one quick glance from the high road, where the Shack could be seen from precisely the right angle. He craned his neck and squinted, but whether in his haste he had passed the correct point on the road or the trees had grown in his absence, he could not see the roof of the factory. He continued along the road to another point from which he was sure the building would be visible; he resolved to hurry to his friends the moment he had had just one glimpse of it.

When he reached the place where he knew he should have a clear view of the Shack, he stopped dead in his tracks to be sure he was not hallucinating. The spot had become unrecognizable. The river's flow had changed completely. Instead of running in a narrow stream along the slope, the water tumbled straight down with a roar that was both fearsome and triumphant. The cliffside, formerly studded with protruding boulders, was now a sheer, clean wall of rock. Where the Shack had stood now lay a forbidding mass of broken stones and uprooted trees that were still green, as if they had just fallen. Buried in this brutal landslide, Sept-Epées's factory had left as little trace as if it had never existed at all.

Sept-Epées's first reaction upon realizing that he was not imagining the disaster before his eyes was to rail against the awful loss of life he was sure the slide must have caused. "Ah! My poor Va-sans-Peur," he cried, stretching his arms involuntarily towards the frightful spectacle. "My workers, my poor apprentices, are you buried here forever?"

"No, thank heaven!" replied a rough voice, and Va-sans-Peur appeared on the road behind him. "We were warned by a monstrous cracking noise that began about two hours before the landslide. We had the time to save ourselves. It happened nearly three weeks ago, and I thought someone would have written to you about it—but in case they hadn't, I have come here each day anticipating your arrival to assure you that at least no one was killed."

"Praise grace," cried Sept-Epées, embracing his overseer. "If you have saved the tools, I may begin my old life again. I have my two hands, and that is all I need."

"I am sorry to tell you, but the tools—and everything else—are gone," admitted Va-sans-Peur. "They were too heavy to carry out. We might have expected something like this—didn't Audebert always say that this place was bewitched by the devil himself?"

"My dear friend," responded Sept-Epées, "the only devil that has ever occupied this place is greed, which leads ambitious men to places where there is no solid ground beneath their feet. If I had known then what I know now, I would never have placed all my hopes in a place that could so easily be destroyed at any moment. All in all, I cannot regret an experience that made me so much wiser and that at least had the happy effect of saving Audebert from debtor's prison, or perhaps an even worse fate. I'm still young, and there is plenty of time for me to rebuild my life. We are free from debt, are we not?"

"Believe it or not, we have collected a profit," said Va-sans-Peur. "Alas! We were operating quite smoothly, but perhaps in the end it will be better for you to find work in the new workshop that has just opened in town. I have already found a place there, and with the talent that you possess I'm sure you will have no shortage of offers. Surely, the new factory was mentioned in the letters you received while you were away?"

"No, there was something else of far more interest to me, and I want you to give me the latest news of it."

Sept-Epées was about to ask for news of Tonine, but as they fell into step together on the road to town he was struck by another strange sight. An old man, completely bald and with a wreath of laurel leaves on his head, walked along the path with a dozen or so children following behind him; he was singing in a broken voice and clapping his hands in a manner at once intent and playful.

"Who is that?" Sept-Epées asked in horror. "Do not tell me it is Audebert, gone crazy!"

"Yes," said Va-sans-Peur, shaking his head sadly. "It has been some time now since he lost his head completely. I blame it on those good-for-nothings in the Upper Town, whom your godfather so rightly despises! They were jealous that the Black City had a better minstrel than all of their young dandies, and they wanted to humiliate him in front of the world. They invited Audebert to some farce they called an 'academic society.' They gave him a banquet, and placed laurel wreaths on his head, and showered him with so many honors and compliments that he came back to us as you see him now. We thought he was drunk, that he would return to normal in the morning, but—well, see for yourself. He has done nothing for three months now but roam the streets in his laurel crown with a pack of children at his heels."

"Poor Audebert!" said Sept-Epées, with tears in his eyes. "That it should end like this! Ah—I did not come home thinking I would find everything in ruins!" He walked toward the old poet, who advanced slowly. Stopping every few steps to recite a verse to the coterie of children, he would place his laurel wreath on the head of one or another of them, then take it back and raise it in the air with gestures of grand enthusiasm.

Va-sans-Peur, seeing that Sept-Epées was weeping, tried to comfort him. "Don't be too distressed by what you see! The old man has never been so happy. He used to have days of sadness, days when he was filled with rage and misery, entire months when he did not work and some friend was obliged to take care of him. Now that he cannot work at all, through no fault of his own, everyone takes very good care of him. I must say this for the Lower Town—wherever he goes, someone gives him something savory to eat or drink. You must see that he is plumper and rosier than ever. He no longer worries that he will be scorned or condemned by others. He is happy, and says only cheerful things now. He spends hours chatting agreeably with the strangers who come to see him—and they come away saying they find nothing wrong with his mind except for the minor detail that he believes he is an ancient troubadour called Pindar! It doesn't harm anyone—and everyone is very careful not to contradict him in his delusion. He is as good a man as he ever was. Not very long ago, he entered a burning house saying the gods would protect him. They say there is one god for lovers, one for drunks, and one for fools—that makes three, and Audebert passed through the flames unharmed and saved a child, who also emerged without a mark on him. That's the child there, the little blond boy clutching Audebert's hand. Some people wanted to call it a miracle, and to them the old man is more a saint than a fool. One thing is certain: dear Audebert always had and always will have a good heart, and it is our duty now to protect him. All of the little children you see around him are his bodyguards. Their parents have told them to make sure no harm comes to him, and if any one of them has the ill grace to insult him, he is chased and soundly thumped by the others. Tomorrow it will be a different group of children—they attend him like he is a school! Indeed, he does teach them valuable things from time to time. Look, he has seen you, and he recognizes you, for he is coming toward you with open arms. Call him Pindar, and everything will go well!"

Sept-Epées clasped the old man to his heart, and saw immediately that Va-sans-Peur had not been mistaken—Audebert was happy. He believed the world had finally done him justice, and having satiated himself with illusions of glory, he had an air of serene modesty. He did call himself Pindar and did wear wreaths of laurel leaves, but that was the extent of his delusion. It seemed that he had heard the name

Pindar in one of the verses addressed to him at the infamous banquet, in which he had been compared to the poet of antiquity. Once he had persuaded himself that he was Pindar returned to earth, he felt it unseemly to continue his work as a knife-maker. As Pindar, he found it only fitting that the townspeople should be willing to honor him by giving him supper and a drink wherever he went. He remained sober in accordance with his newfound sense of dignity, and his benefactors were so numerous that he could enter a different house each night without exhausting his welcome.

Audebert spoke to Sept-Epées in the most cordial manner, if a bit vaguely, but with obvious contentment and without seeming in the least unaware of reality. "You have lost the factory," he said. "The mountain has taken its revenge upon us. I see that you are bearing this misfortune with courage and wisdom, and you are right to do so. Happiness does not lie in a pile of stones, and you are not destined to be the slave of a machine any more than I am. True happiness is waiting for you, the happiness of love and friendship, and that is why I will be on my way now—you must be anxious to reunite with your loved ones!" He embraced Sept-Epées again and continued along the path, children in tow.

"Let us hurry," said Sept-Epées to his companion. "I'm long overdue! And yet, I wonder if you should not go ahead and tell my friends that I'm coming. I fear that Tonine—"

"Bah! Tonine!" interrupted Va-sans-Peur with a shrug. "Are you still thinking of her? You are not as reasonable as I thought!"

"What do you mean?" asked Sept-Epées. "Oh—yes, I understand. You think she is ill, poor, in debt—and that I, poor now as well, have come home to wed misery to misery? You're wrong, my friend! Misery does not exist for a man who has courage and a little talent, and nothing is impossible for those who love."

"You speak to me about things of which I know nothing," returned the other man. "You would be better off remaining ignorant as well. But look—here comes Lise to meet you, and whatever you have in mind it does not concern me. I will leave the two of you together."

Lise had her three children with her. Rosette was a head taller than she had been the last time Sept-Epées had seen her, and she was groomed just as prettily as she had been when Tonine used to brush her blond curls and pleat her little white collar. Lise, too, looked extremely well; she seemed rejuvenated.

Sept-Epées embraced Lise. "You look very well," he said. "That at least is some consolation. It gives me a bit of hope for Tonine."

"Tonine has improved since she heard you were coming home," said Lise. "She is even strong enough to have gone outside for a bit today, if carried in a chair. You may see her in a couple of hours."

"What? She is well enough to go out, and she didn't ask to be brought to meet me?"

"How were we to know what road you would take?" returned Lise. "We have waited for you so long that we did not know what to think! At any rate, you will not find her at home yet, and we have the time to talk a little. I must rest a bit—I'm tired from carrying the baby so far."

Lise sat on the grass, the infant in her lap.

"You're worrying me, Lise," said Sept-Epées. "Tonine's illness is worse, or she is terribly changed, and you are trying to prepare me for it."

"If Tonine was worse, I would not be here with you," replied Lise. "As to whether she is changed—if that were true, my friend, if she had become ugly, or lost her beautiful hair, if her illness had aged her prematurely, what would you say? What would you do then?"

CHAPTER XIV

Sept-Epées had not considered the possibilities Lise was setting before him. He turned pale, but his resolve did not waver. "Lise," he said, "I have tried for a long time to hide the fact that I'm love with Tonine. I cannot deny it any longer. I have loved her with both my heart and my mind, knowing that there is no other woman as wise and good as she is. I do not believe the memory of her face has been the chief cause of my regrets, but neither can I tell you how I will feel if that lovely face has changed, for I don't know myself. If Tonine has become an invalid, she will perhaps be quite different, but even if that is so it will not alter my feelings. I came back to offer her what little money I believed I had. Now I know I have nothing but the strength and the desire to work, and I would rather work myself to death than see Tonine suffer. I want nothing more than to give her more than she would ever be able to repay. These are my thoughts, Lise. What do you say?"

"Calm yourself, my friend," said Lise, taking his hand. "Tonine is not an invalid, nor has she been disfigured by her illness. I wanted to know if your friendship for her was genuine, and I see now that you deserve hers. Let us go now, and find her. Carry my little one, if you do not mind, and we will travel faster."

Lise walked ahead of Sept-Epées, but instead of entering the maze of twisting passages that made up the Black City, she turned left down a footpath that had been cut into the rock; it had not been there before.

"I see that we have a new road that will make traveling around town much easier," remarked Sept-Epées.

"Yes, and it is pleasing to us parents as well. We no longer fear seeing our children crushed by the wheels of carriages on the main roads that stretch to our very doorsteps. Our homes are much safer now—and much cleaner of road dust as well."

"There does seem to be a sort of Sunday aura about the place," mused Sept-Epées, "even though it is the middle of the week. But why are you taking me along this route? I would rather see my friends than take time to admire the local improvements!"

"I have my reasons for going this way, dear friend! You will find neither Gaucher nor Laguerre at the Trottin workshop. They are at the Barre-Molino factory now."

"Indeed? What would possess them to leave a decent employer to work under a harsh and sometimes unfair one?"

"The overseer? He is no longer there since Molino died."

"Molino—dead? I didn't know any of this had taken place! Are his heirs, then, a little kinder than he was?"

"He has only one heir," said Lise. "A young woman. Do you not know of her?"

"Why, no!" cried Sept-Epées. "Did Molino have a daughter? I did not know he had any family in these parts."

"It does not matter," returned Lise. "She's nothing like him—in fact, she is a great deal like Tonine. She thinks only of the welfare of others. She is responsible for the construction of the road we are traveling on, which has been such a great improvement for the Lower Town. You will scarcely recognize the Barre-Molino place. It is a perfect cooperative. Its profits have been spectacular, and nearly all of the money goes to provide free education and apprenticeships to the children of the Black City, to care for the sick, to train workers, and to compensate those who have been injured while working. You will see public baths and classrooms, and you will be proud to work there, whether as a worker—or a teacher—or overseer."

"All of this is wonderful, Lise!" Sept-Epées exclaimed. "It's high time that the Black City, like other villages I encountered in my travels, be blessed with a benefactor. She must be very rich, this young woman, to sacrifice so much of her income for the welfare of the rest of us."

"She isn't rich, exactly. She inherited only the factory and a sum of money that she immediately used to build this road and establish the cooperative. She thinks very little of herself—she lives as simply as any young working woman. You will see! Your godfather and Gaucher and I all think very highly of her, and we will introduce you to her today. Tomorrow you can begin working to help Tonine as you said you wished to do."

"I am grateful to you and the others, but I thought you

would let me see Tonine right away! She cannot be working at the knife shop! Look, here we are at the Laurentis house."

"She does not live there any more," said Lise, "but Madame Laurentis has kept her room vacant so that she can return, if she chooses."

"And she is there now, I'm sure of it!" cried Sept-Epées, handing the baby to his mother. "Do you see, the window is open!" He launched himself along the smooth new path, vaulted over the low railing that protected her pots of wildflowers, and bounded across the terrace.

Tonine was indeed there. She had heard him coming. She threw herself into his arms, and the two were so overjoyed at seeing one another again that for a moment neither of them could speak through their tears. They finally drew back a little, and looked each other over. Sept-Epées was, more than ever, the handsomest young man in the village. His face had taken on a stronger, more masculine quality, yet it had also softened. Everything he had suffered, lost, and learned was written on his features. A new keenness glittered in his eyes; one sensed that he had seen and understood many things, and that he had experienced emotion to the very depths of his soul.

As for Tonine, the face that had never been exactly beautiful was now undeniably, radiantly lovely. She had lost her pallor, and the contours of her face and body had assumed a healthier fullness without losing their delicacy. Her dress was much as it had always been, simple and elegant, but a slightly more generous cut to her skirt, and the heightened sheen and curl in her hair lent her even more of the indefinable royal air that she had always possessed.

"You have been misled, my dear friend," she said to Sept-Epées. "I was never ill, nor in despair. Lise made all of it up so that you would come home, and I did nothing to stop her. Can you forgive me?"

"Tonine, I should thank you! You knew I would come. But why did you not summon me sooner?"

"Why did you not return when I wrote to you that I would not marry Doctor Anthime?"

"Did you write that to me, Tonine?" cried the young man.

"Yes, three days after you left—as soon as I found out you had gone."

"I never received the letter! Ah, what poor luck! To have suffered so much, believing you were lost to me forever, when happiness could have been ours so soon!"

Tonine shook her head. "You must not regret anything. I would not have married you right away, and, who knows—it might have taken me some time to trust you again. We did not understand each other at the time, don't you see? We could not have understood each other. There were too many things weighing on your mind, and I wasn't thinking very clearly myself. I had my own ambitions. I wanted to better the lives of everyone around me, and I didn't believe your regard for me was sincere. I must confess something to you, Sept-Epées. When I thought you would marry Clarisse Trottin, I tried to make myself care for another as well, but I could not force myself to love him. When I heard that you were in distress, I could not pretend any longer. I told Doctor

Anthime that I was grateful to him for his regard, but that I had always loved you, in spite of myself, and that I loved you still—you, and not him. We parted with a handshake. Since then, I have believed that you had forgotten me completely, and I tried not to think of you any longer, but I could not bring myself to look at anyone else. I hid my longing and my sadness. I tried to keep myself occupied with large projects that I will tell you about later, and I thought I would never have the leisure to marry. But when Gaucher showed me your letter, I learned not only that you were gentler and wiser, but that you still loved me as well. And when the accident happened with the factory, I suddenly knew that I must unburden my heart to Lise, and tell her that I wanted you to come home. She invented a scheme to make you believe I was ill, and, you see—everything has worked out for the best. You were tired of traveling, and ready to marry."

"And we will be married, will we not, Tonine? We will be married right away! I know that I'm ruined, and that if you have not really been ill, then you do not need me—and I know you could likely find someone a great deal better than me. You are so good that you might marry me simply to help me out of my poverty, but I don't care! I swear to you, Tonine, that if you are not my wife soon, I will go mad!"

"Then we'd better hurry and announce the engagement!" laughed Tonine. She turned to Lise, who had maintained a discreet distance with the children. "Did you hear? He has proposed, and we have pledged ourselves to one another! Let us go now and share the good news with Laguerre and Gaucher. Give me the baby, Lise, for he weighs you down too much. Sept-Epées can carry your other little one, and Rosette runs nearly as fast as we do."

Taking the children, Tonine and Sept-Epées exchanged an involuntary glance at the realization that they might one day know the joy of holding an infant born of their own union. They began walking rapidly through the narrow streets of the Black City, but they were stopped numerous times by townspeople wishing to welcome Sept-Epées home from his travels and hear tales of his adventures. The young man assured them that he would tell them everything at a later time, and when Tonine stepped in to help him disengage himself he was struck by the deference with which everyone treated her. The esteem in which she had always been held seemed to have changed into a deeper respect, and Sept-Epées felt his heart swell with pride that this paragon of virtue and morality had agreed to become his wife.

Continuing down along the riverbank, they passed underneath a large new arcade, which was also, evidently, the work of the mysterious "mademoiselle," and Sept-Epées found himself suddenly facing a huge factory that he instantly recognized as the Barre-Molino, so agreeably remodeled that it seemed more a place of relaxation than of work. The rumbling waterwheels, growling like so many trapped lions under the lower arcades, divided the river into a thousand tiny streams flowing across the plain—for this immense factory reached into the countryside. Situated at the foot of a sheltering cliff, fortified against the fiercest of storms, the place preserved an air of tranquility in the valley that stretched out before it in a vast checkerboard of green and gold.

"Good Lord!" exclaimed Sept-Epées. "Someone has taken this sad old carcass of a place and transformed it into a palace, and if the inside is as grand as the outside, our sooty companions must be like smudges in the sunlight!"

"Go in," responded Lise, "and you will see them as well situated as they would be anywhere you might have visited during your travels."

Sept-Epées passed through a series of clean, bright rooms where the tired, sweaty workers spent their periods of rest sheltered from heat or cold. He saw a nursery where children played in an orderly fashion, as they were supervised by a worker known for his benevolent nature. Madame Sauvière, the mother of Tonine's friend Rosalie, stood by in case anyone complained of illness or exhaustion. Finally, they arrived at the forge, where Laguerre worked busily. The old man had not been told that his godson was coming home. His surprise and happiness shone in his eyes, and he tossed his tools aside and hugged this prodigal son to his chest until he was sure that Sept-Epées was no illusion. Gaucher, summoned by Lise, showed the same astonished pleasure at seeing his friend—the two women had kept their secret well.

"You find us very well and happy," Gaucher assured Sept-Epées. "We have both been hired as overseers, and a man could not ask for a better situation. You will certainly receive the choicest position in the entire place—no one is more knowledgeable and full of ideas than you."

"No doubt, no doubt," added Laguerre fondly. "And let us

hope that you are never tempted to leave us again, you rascal!"

"Never!" cried Sept-Epées. "No, never again—I am going to marry Tonine!"

"Can it be possible?" exclaimed Gaucher, whose shock was reflected on Laguerre's stunned face.

"My son," said the old man at last, "have you lost your mind? You—marry Tonine? Now?"

Sept-Epées, taken aback, scanned the room for Tonine, who had disappeared. "Do you know of some reason why I should not marry her?" he asked his godfather.

"You must be joking to ask me that! I have had enough of jokes. Are you trying to make us both look ridiculous? Please, let us talk of something else. Tell us of your—"

"He will tell you everything you want to know," interrupted Lise, who had just come back into the room, "but first he needs to eat something! Mademoiselle has invited us all to dine with her—is that not true, Father Laguerre? Go and get dressed. I will take Sept-Epées back to our house so that he can wash up a bit. It is nearly three o'clock already."

Sept-Epées followed Lise mechanically into a spacious, tidy cottage now occupied by the Gaucher household; it stood not far from the dwellings of Laguerre and Audebert, who required a residence when his troubadour fantasies did not lead him elsewhere. Lise showed the young man into a vacant room. She had already spoken to the mysterious "mademoiselle," she said, and Sept-Epées had been readily granted a job on Lise's and Tonine's recommendations.

Sept-Epées barely heard what his friend was saying.

"That's good," he responded distractedly. "This 'mademoiselle' obviously has a kind heart, and I thank her very sincerely. But—why did Laguerre receive the news of my marriage to Tonine with such ill grace?"

"He was not pleased?"

"His words made me think he did not approve of the idea. There is something more to this, Lise, something you have not told me."

"What more could there be? Perhaps your godfather has simply forgotten what it's like to be in love."

Lise seemed to be embarrassed, and she answered his questions evasively. Worry began to overtake him, and it increased after she had left him alone to change his clothes. He noticed that she lingered in the passageway near his room, as if she intended to prevent him from communicating with anyone outside. He grew more and more troubled in his mind. Had Tonine done something wrong? Had she accidentally become involved in some sort of scandal? She could not possibly have lost her good reputation, not in view of the respect she had received from everyone they had encountered on the street that day—but how else to explain Laguerre's reaction to his announcement of their engagement? And why had Tonine disappeared so suddenly—as if she did not want to be present when Sept-Epées told their friends the news?

CHAPTER XV

When a dark thought enters even as logical a mind as the one possessed by Sept-Epées, it is often all too easy for it to take hold there. The young man began to imagine that Tonine had perhaps had reasons other than emotional ones for calling him back to her side. Why had she not dared to write to him herself? Why had she enlisted Lise's help while concealing her actions from Gaucher and Laguerre? And why had he been told so many lies involving illness, poverty, and disfigurement—as if his devotion was being put to the test? His mind was flooded with images of Tonine: beautiful, laughing, passionate, tolerant Tonine, Tonine accepting his proposal when she had always rejected the idea of marriage, Tonine calling upon Lise to witness their engagement and then hurrying across town to this astonishing new workplace. Had she played him for a fool from the first? Gaucher had certainly seemed shocked by the idea of his marrying Tonine—and had not Va-sans-Peur told him on the mountainside that it was "impossible" that he should still care for her?

Sept-Epées dressed himself distractedly and sank into a

chair without a thought that there were people waiting for him. His glance, moving restlessly around the room, fell upon an object on the windowsill—a pot of forget-me-nots; a blue and white pot he knew very well. He had discovered that same pot of flowers in his chamber at the Laurentis rooming house the day that Tonine had supervised his installation there. She knew he was fond of the scent of forget-me-nots. She had always been discreetly attentive to his tastes.

Sept-Epées felt tears slide down his burning cheeks. There was a mystery swirling around him, and he felt sure that it boded ill. How had Tonine known that he would be invited to dine by "mademoiselle," and how had she known that he would be shown to precisely this empty chamber to change his clothes? This mademoiselle who was so generous and good—was she too good, perhaps? Did she have a brother, or a nephew? No, no! Sept-Epées shook his head violently and tried to clear it of such disturbing thoughts. He was letting his imagination run away with him—Tonine was an angel! Tonine, Lise! Tonine, Gaucher! Where were they? Why had he been left alone in such an agony of confusion?

"Here we are!" Louis Gaucher's cheerful voice broke into his thoughts. He and Lise were standing in the doorway. "Tonine is waiting for us. Your godfather and our other friends should be there as well. Let us go quickly—we are already a bit late."

"My friend," said Sept-Epées, linking his arm through Gaucher's, "I don't know where you're taking me, but the honesty in your eyes gives me courage."

"We are taking you to meet mademoiselle, our patron, our

friend," said Lise, who followed them with the children. "There are a dozen of us who dine with her each Sunday, and today is indeed Sunday for us, because you have come home."

"But what can my return possibly mean to this unknown mademoiselle?"

Gaucher laughed. "Anyone who is dear to us, is dear to her as well."

They crossed a small wooden footbridge that stretched over a narrow, calm bend in the river. The bridge was connected to a tiny island set in the smooth-flowing water and blanketed with carefully tended flowers whose brilliant colors were reflected in the river's mirror-like surface. The modest home of the mysterious "mademoiselle," a simple two-story structure with three large windows on each level, stood among the rosebushes. Obviously the solid work of local stonemasons, it was fenced by hedges of lilac and painted a soft pearl gray. The place was so simply designed and built that any qualified worker might have constructed it, but its clean lines and lovely surroundings gave it such an air of peace and repose that anyone would have been pleased to live there. The slope of the small bit of land upon which it stood was steep enough to prevent any possibility of flooding, and a circle of pines and shrubs protected the little house from the valley's fierce winds.

A pathway of black gravel led to the house's front entry. A small dog trotted out to greet the visitors as they approached; its bark brought the rosy-cheeked, smiling face of Madame Laurentis to one of the first-floor windows.

"Mademoiselle has given Madame Laurentis the job of running her entire household," said Gaucher to Sept-Epées. "She is an unparalleled cook, as you well know, and has quite a way with an omelet."

They entered the living room, which, like the dining room, was designed to accommodate a dozen people comfortably. It was furnished in soft fabrics and bright woods, and boasted white muslin curtains, pots of colorful flowers, and a beautiful old table that Sept-Epées thought he remembered seeing in Tonine's rooms.

Laguerre was there already—and Rosalie Sauvière and her mother, and Doctor Anthime, and Va-sans-Peur. Audebert was expected as well, but he had declared that poets were not bound by the clock and they should not wait for him. Tonine arrived last, dressed entirely in white and so radiantly lovely that Sept-Epées felt his breath leave him at the sight of her. She came to him and took his hands, laughing. Everyone else in the room laughed with her, and Sept-Epées thought to himself that Laguerre had been right. He laughed as well, in an attempt to appear as carefree as the others, but his laughter ceased suddenly when he caught sight of Doctor Anthime. Rosalie Sauvière, looking healthy and attractive in well-cut clothes, noted the direction of his gaze.

"Why, what's the matter?" she said to Sept-Epées. "You are looking at my husband as if you had never seen him before. Why have you not yet greeted him?"

"Your husband?" exclaimed Sept-Epées, fighting a sudden impulse to embrace the doctor.

"Yes," said Anthime. "I seem to have been destined to

settle here in the Black City. One worthy young woman refused my proposal, but I soon met another, a lovely patient of mine, who was grateful for my care and repaid me by giving me her hand in marriage. I'm the factory doctor now, my dear fellow, but from the looks of you, you will not soon have any need of my services."

"Everyone to the table!" cried Madame Laurentis from the kitchen, and the little dog, who seemed quite familiar with this announcement, trotted around the guests' feet, while barking happily and herding them into the dining room.

Anthime offered his arm to Tonine, who stepped aside to let Laguerre proceed to the table. Madame Anthime took Sept-Epées's arm, and the others followed.

The dining room was as clean and comfortable as the living room. A variety of simple, hearty dishes had been set out on a white tablecloth embroidered with violets. There was something matriarchal about the atmosphere of hospitality in the house. All of the guests were served at the same time, and Madame Laurentis took her place at the table after she had finished passing the plates.

Tonine sat down in the place of honor, with Laguerre across from her, the doctor on her right, and Sept-Epées on her left. "Mademoiselle" had not thus far made her appearance; it was almost as if she did not exist. Sept-Epées could not resist mentioning this to Madame Anthime, who was seated next to him. "Oh," she replied, "she will appear later, after the meal."

"No," interrupted Tonine. "She will appear right away. We have deceived my fiancé long enough, and I can see that he is becoming uncomfortable. Sept-Epées, my beloved, do not wait for mademoiselle any longer—she is already here. It is I, I who sit here speaking to you, and I who ask your forgiveness for creating this confusion."

"You!" cried the young man incredulously, still a bit uneasy. "You—mademoiselle? The heiress?"

"Yes—I, Tonine, who is today your fiancée and tomorrow will be your wife. Are you not going to do as your godfather did, and say that this is impossible? It is more than possible, because we are in love, you and I, and you've given me your word. My friends," she continued, turning to the others, "you do not all know what has happened. Madame Gaucher and I made our friend believe that I was ill, poor, and desperately unhappy, and we even told him that my looks had been ruined by my misfortune. He rushed to my side, still determined to marry me, even in the face of such adversity, believing he could give me a comfortable life without even knowing what had happened to his factory. I ask all of you for your opinion—am I right to trust him, to want to be his wife?"

"Yes, yes!" the entire room burst forth. "Yes!" repeated a voice from the doorway, which proved to be that of Audebert. "Ah, house of love," he continued, "I lift my wreath to this place, which is surely watched over by the gods!"

Tonine crossed to Audebert. "My friend," she said, taking the laurel wreath from his hand, "bless this day by allowing us the honor of your dignified presence. Give me the laurel wreath; you do not need it. Promise me that you will not wear it again."

"I promise," replied Audebert solemnly. "I will no longer wear the laurel—I promise—I promise."

"And I accept this sign of your friendship with gratitude," Tonine said to him. "This laurel wreath has gained you the respect and friendship of the people of the Black City. It shall remain here as a tribute to you."

"You are right, young muse!" exclaimed Audebert. "I have perhaps acted foolishly in continuing to wear this symbol of my triumph. Allow me to join you at the table, my friends. I will sing to you in celebration of the happy couple."

"But we haven't had dessert!" protested Laguerre, who did not always care for his old friend's poetry. "And besides, we have serious matters to speak of. What do you think of all this, my dear godson?"

"I am happy," responded Sept-Epées simply. "I'm going to marry Tonine, whom I have always loved, and that is enough. Rich or poor, she is Tonine, and that is all that matters. Her new fortune and station in life did not make her the woman she is."

"A lovely thought," observed Doctor Anthime. "But allow me to remind you that wealth—which the two of you will share, once you are married—adds greatly to happiness, if you use it wisely and generously, as Tonine has done."

"I have no other wish but Tonine's," said Sept-Epées. "Speak to me, then, my dear. The good fortune you always deserved has found you at last, and there is proof that luck is not blind. I cannot share your wealth, it is true, if I do not share your feelings as well."

"Well, then," responded Tonine, "let me tell you how I

came to be my brother-in-law's heiress, and you will understand our duty. Do you remember that Molino was ill when you left town? He had abused his health, and he knew he was dying. He regretted his past. He asked to see me and then begged my pardon for the fate of my poor sister. I agreed to forgive him, on the condition that he do something charitable for the needy residents of the Black City. He promised to do so, and I took care of him until he succumbed to his illness. When his will was read, we were all astonished to hear that he had left the factory to me. There were a few conditions to his request, however. For one, I was to do what I could to make up for the offenses his overseer had inflicted on the factory's workers. The result, my dear Sept-Epées, was what you have seen today. I hope I have fulfilled my obligation before God. We must each do what we can for the good of our souls."

"Do not worry, my dear," said Sept-Epées reassuringly. "I don't know if I can ever truly match your goodness, but I'm a proud man, and I don't think I could live if you were not proud of me as well."

During dinner, Sept-Epées noticed that Tonine had indeed changed since the last time he saw her. She had always had a spirit to match his, but it had been obvious that she knew little of life beyond her own unhappy childhood. She had freely admitted her ignorance of the more practical aspects of life that were so important to Sept-Epées. With her inheritance, however, Tonine's horizons had broadened considerably. She had devoted herself to studying the art and science of the industry that she now governed, and without ever leaving the valley she had become quite knowledgeable about the industrial and commercial movement in France.

Sept-Epées found a great deal of pleasure in speaking, both in front of Tonine and with her, about everything he had seen and learned, without needing to explain concepts and terms that would have been foreign to her in the past. He was proud to be able to tell her of procedures he had seen and of ideas and concepts that could be used to improve local conditions, and he was proud to see his thoughts and notions fully understood and appreciated by her quick intellect, which played so important a role in implementing the desires of her devoted heart.

CHAPTER XVI

The marriage banns were published the following day, and the sunrise found Sept-Epées working in the new factory. He had chosen to begin as a simple laborer, out of his desire to demonstrate his respect for manual work. He worked even more swiftly and surely than ever, and quickly won the esteem of those who would soon be under his supervision. He taught an evening course in basic metalwork and showed himself to be a skilled instructor. When class was over, he mingled with his friends, who were eager to celebrate his return, and his unfailing kindness and sincerity proved him to be a devoted friend and brother.

Tonine had wanted their wedding to be no more elaborate than any other village artisan's, but she did not anticipate the enthusiasm of the Black City's inhabitants. Local children spent eight days gathering a veritable mountain of flowers and wove them into immense garlands and triumphal arches under which the wedding procession passed. The number of friends and well-wishers in the procession itself became so enormous that it seemed as if a civil celebration was taking place. After the ceremony, a great banquet was held on the banks of the river. Each family brought its own repast, and everyone ate, sang, and made merry while the young newlyweds, surrounded by their intimate friends and family, dined under the lilacs on the tiny island where they would make their home; the endless toasts given and received echoed throughout the natural amphitheatre afforded by the valley. A group of young boys, garlanded with wreaths of flowers, drew a handmade chariot, upon which Sept-Epées and his bride made a tour of the festival grounds, there to receive handshakes and more congratulations. Tonine was persuaded to open the dancing, and when she did everyone observed that it was the first time she had ever been seen to dance in public. She moved so gracefully to the music that all present marveled at her skill and admired her restraint, for having refrained for so long from displaying her talents.

During the celebrations, Tonine stopped dancing several times to ask if anyone had seen Audebert. Capricious as he was, the old poet never forgot his friends, and they found it very odd that he was absent on such an occasion. Just as they had begun to worry about him, however, he suddenly appeared on an outcropping of rock that provided a welcome bit of shade to the revelers. With him stood Saviero, or Xavier, an Italian plasterer with a magical singing voice who had recently arrived in the area to craft frescoes and statuary in the municipal buildings of the Upper Town. The young man had a noticeable accent when he sang, but his voice was so lovely that one noticed only an added clarity of enunciation in his verses. From his rocky vantage point, Audebert made what was evidently a rehearsed gesture with a fresh green twig. The factory's sluices, silenced for the celebration, came to life with a roaring rush of water reminiscent of the pounding of hammers, at the same time as the glowing furnaces sent spirals of smoke into the clear air.

It was a grand and awe-inspiring simulation of the sounds of work in the factory, and it provided the overture to Audebert's cantata. Descending with Saviero to a lower outcropping of rock that brought the two performers suitably close to the waiting audience, Audebert gave another sign and the music of the sluices ceased. The waterfalls were contained as if by magic, and a choir of workers sang the opening notes of the old poet's grandest composition yet. By turns, Saviero recited and sang the verses and the chorus, and everyone agreed that Audebert's work had never been so inspired. His generous heart had provided an outlet for his troubled genius, and if there was a fault or two to be found in the language of his verses, the paraphrase in prose with which we now close our true narrative will show that his ideas were as priceless in their sentiment as they were flawless in their beauty.

CHORUS

Terrible storms, quiet! Raging river, quiet! Iron and flame, chisels and hammers, thunderous labor, silence! Today we sing a song of love; today is a day for rejoicing.

RECITATION

You, young husband, adopted son of the Black City, receive the blessing of friendship; it is the blessing of God upon your love. Hear, in the voice of an unknown friend, the wisdom of old age. Experience holds truth and knowledge, for behind it stretch long days of hope and despair, of pleasure and pain. Experience cries out, "Remember!"

VERSES

O yes—remember days gone by. They fly quickly, but their lessons remain. The rigors of your apprenticeship, the first tests of your strength, the dreams of your spirit, and the sufferings of your heart—all have already taught you what a boy must endure to become a man, and what a man must understand to become an elder. Remember!

Remember the day the waters rose, the trees fell, and the machines of steel ground to a halt in the face of nature's ferocity. Your elder encouraged you, and pointed with a smile to the small birds attempting their first flights from nests clinging to storm-ravaged limbs. And you, you smiled in your turn, not wishing to be less courageous than the tiny winged ones. Remember!

Remember the first accidental blow of the hammer, when metal bruised your poor flesh. It was your first cry, your first blood. You were baptized on that day, and your elder told you: "Calm yourself, it is nothing—it is a mother's kiss!" And you took up your hammer again, and said: "Soon, I shall lead the leader." Remember!

Remember the first finished product to come from your hands. Pride visited you that day, and you felt your chest swell with pride. You came from the dark of the forge to the brilliance of sunlight, seeking an errant beam to illuminate the steel worked by your hand, and it seemed that the entire world was watching you, saying: "The child is gone—a man now stands among us!" Remember!

Remember the day when your purse was full, and you saw the world open before you. The limitless future was yours that day, and you had only to choose your path. But while your dreams were grand, your station was yet low, and your struggle had only begun. You began the long road to mastery of machines, ponderous and delicate, acquiescent and rebellious, generous and ungrateful—and finally, the machine of all machines, a man who works for another man. Remember!

Remember the day where you felt at odds with the world—with your friends, your family, even with yourself? You realized that day that in order to succeed, you would have to open yourself completely; you would find that your trust was misplaced, your heart broken, your compassion exploited, your friendship unappreciated—and on that day, you threw aside your tools and you wept. You learned that men are men, and that ambition of iron requires patience of steel. Remember!

Remember the day when your heart gained mastery over your spirit, and you knew you could bend destiny to your will. On that day, you reconciled with your friends, with God, with yourself. On that day, you saw that the heat and flame of the forge did not come from Hell, and you heard in the roar of the river the word of God. You felt a new vigor in your blood that came from Heaven itself. Remember!

And today, a day you will remember above all others, remember that science is a treasure, and that life has taught you many things that are unknown to those who have not suffered—and remember one thing above all others: happiness does not lie in the triumph of an isolated will, but in a combination of wills dedicated to doing good. And remember also that love means more than reason, and that life itself exists because of love. Never forget that—always remember it. Remember!

CHORUS

And now, rage, terrible storms! Roar and rumble, powerful river! Fire and flame, hammer and chisel, thunder of man's labor, give way to the dance! You cannot drown the music of love. Today is a day for rejoicing!

Here the assembled listeners burst into applause, and after

the singer had taken advantage of the moment to rest, silence descended once more, as everyone awaited the verses dedicated to the bride. The chorus was heard again:

> *You, beautiful bride, daughter of the Black City!*
> *Receive the blessing of friendship; it is the blessing of God upon your love*

Once again, Saviero's voice boomed forth the recitation:

> *Hear, in the voice of an unknown friend, the wisdom of old age. Experience holds truth and knowledge, for behind it stretch long days of hope and despair, of pleasure and pain. Experience cries out, "Remember!"*

VERSES

You, who were blessed at birth, Tonine, with your white hands, remember the first day that your mother took you into the mountains. You saw a flower turning its face to the sun, and you ran to cut it. For you it was the loveliest of all flowers, a gift from the earth—it was the first time you understood the meaning of beauty. Your sister, older than you, wanted the flower as well, and instead of crying, you gave it to her with a smile. That was the first time you knew the joy of giving, greater for you than all other pleasures. Remember!

You, who were blessed as you grew up, Tonine, with your capable hands, remember the first day you entered the workshop to earn the poor wages of a child. You were an orphan, and you had forgotten how to laugh. The overseer asked: "Who is this pale girl who asks for nothing, who never seems to know weariness, who shows such skill and patience despite her tender years?" And the response he received was: "She is a girl who does the work of two, because her sister is weighed down with sorrow, and though she is the younger, she is the more closely united with God." Remember!

You, who were blessed with beauty, Tonine, with your graceful hands, remember the day you were asked to your first dance. The floor was prepared; the violins were ready to play their loveliest melodies. All of the young men were there, and you were invited to put on your loveliest white dress and follow them. One day of pleasure, they said, would erase a year of sorrow. No, you said, they did not need your company to enjoy themselves, and you went to spend the evening with Louisa, the box-maker, who lived alone. You put on your white dress, and made a sick woman happy for a few hours. Remember!

You, who were blessed with saintly goodness, Tonine, with your gentle hands, remember the day you gave your bread and water away to a poor traveler, and the day you promised not to turn in a friendless, penniless thief if only he would seek help for his soul. Remember the day you cared for a poor cripple who had been abandoned by his own family, and the day you gave away your coat, the day you gave away your shoes, and finally, with nothing left to give, the day you gave away your tears. Remember all the days you consecrated with good deeds, devotion, and sacrifices—remember all these days, Tonine, with your lovely hands. Remember!

Now remember, Tonine, with your pure heart, the day when they said to you: "You are rich, and the grandest factory in the Black City is yours." That day, you raised your hands to the sky and said: "Nothing is mine, all belongs to the Lord!" And since that day, Tonine, there has been no sorrow here that has not been healed, no tear that has not been dried. Remember!

And remember, Tonine, with your loyal heart, the day when they said to you: "The factory owned by the man who loves you is gone, devoured by the mountain. Everything he had has been buried in a tumble of stone; the river sings its cruel victory over the ruins of his work and his life." On that day, you cried to yourself: "My fiancé is coming home, summoned by the sound of my voice. I am in need of a companion to help bear the responsibility of wealth." On that day, Tonine, with your tender heart, you loved someone else more than yourself, someone who had nothing left but his faith in the bounty of the earth. Remember!

RECITATION

Young newlyweds, remember the weariness and pain

you have endured to better savor the richness of joy! Noble children of toil, never leave the Black City! Bonds stronger than fine tempered steel, affection more solid than the granite boulders that protect our sanctuary of industry, bonds of love and friendship shall keep you here. Our black cavern may seem inhospitable to the stranger passing by, but we who have lived our lives in the midst of smoke and flames know that our hearts are as passionate as anyone's! Remember these hearts, young newlyweds. Remember them forever!

CHORUS

And now, rage, terrible storms! Roar and rumble, powerful river! Fire and flame, hammer and chisel, thunder of man's labor, give way to the dance! You cannot drown the music of love. Today is a day for rejoicing!

The thunderous applause of the people of the Black City echoed off the walls of the gorge. Suddenly it was joined by another noise, one that seemed to come from nowhere. All eyes turned to the mountain and saw an enormous crowd of people, clapping their hands and waving their handkerchiefs. They were the workers and businessmen, the young and old bourgeois of the Upper Town, singing and descending toward the riverbank.

The news had spread to the Upper Town that a grand wedding was to take place that day in the Lower Town, and

Tonine had acquired her reputation as an angel in both places. Molino's will had drawn a great deal of attention to her. No one had wanted to embarrass the modest young woman by congratulating her too warmly on her upcoming nuptials, but when the people of the Upper Town saw the factory's smokestacks and sluices working on a Sunday they knew immediately that something special was occurring. They had not been able to make out the words of the cantata, but the voices of Saviero and Audebert had immediately told them what was happening. They had swarmed down the mountain to pay their respects to the young couple, and, as the applause following the cantata was lengthy, there had been plenty of time for everyone to settle comfortably.

That day, on the expanse of green grass that marked the separation of ravine and plain, two towns, sisters and rivals, mingled cordially in one immense celebration. All disagreements, prejudices, and quarrels vanished into the air. Old friendships were renewed, and old wounds were soothed by the magical sounds of the flute and the violin. Laguerre, flattered by the unexpected politeness of the people he had always scorned, declared that even if the Black City would always be the seat of wisdom and virtue, perhaps there was also something to be said for its neighbor, after all.

"I have two cats," said Emma.
"And a dog. But they are old.
All they do is sleep.
They won't hurt Fluffy."

So Fluffy went home with Emma.
“The brown cat is Jack,” Emma told Fluffy.
“The orange one is Jill.”
Nice kitties, thought Fluffy.

“This is Skippy,” Emma said.
Woof! Woof! thought Fluffy.

That night, Emma and Fluffy
had a tea party.
Then Fluffy went to sleep under his straw.

In the middle of the night,

Fluffy heard a noise.

He opened his eyes.

Four big yellow eyes were looking at him.

Yikes! thought Fluffy.

I'm having a bad dream!

But it wasn't a dream.

It was Jack and Jill.

Don't mess with me, cats, said Fluffy.

Jack patted the door of Fluffy's cage
with his paw.
The door opened.
You are asking for trouble, said Fluffy.

Jill poked her paw into the cage
and pulled Fluffy out the door.
You'll be sorry! said Fluffy.

Jill picked Fluffy up and
carried him into the living room.
She put him down on the floor.
I have sharp teeth, Fluffy told Jack.
Jack showed Fluffy his sharp teeth.
I have sharp claws, Fluffy told Jill.
Jill stuck out her sharp claws.

Okay, cats, said Fluffy. **Look out!**

Fluffy ran at Jill.

He jumped at Jack.

He ran and jumped and growled.

Fluffy did not see Skippy come up behind him.

But Jack and Jill did.

Their eyes got very big and they ran away.

I told you not to mess with me, cats!

Fluffy called after them.

Then Fluffy turned around.

He saw Skippy.

Don't be afraid, Skippy, said Fluffy.

I scared the cats away.

Fluffy did not know
how to get back to his cage.
So he followed Skippy to his bed.
Fluffy lay down beside the dog.
Wake me up if the cats come back,
Fluffy told Skippy.
I will take care of them.
Then Fluffy the Brave fell asleep.

Fluffy the Explorer

"I'm going to get a haircut,"
Emma told Fluffy.
"Dad says you can come, too."
Why? said Fluffy. **My hair is just right.**
Emma put Fluffy in a shoe box
and off they went.

They walked into Sandy's Haircuts.

"Will you watch Fluffy?" Emma asked.

"Sure," said her dad.

Emma went to get her hair washed.

Her dad sat down.

He put the shoe box on a chair.

Then he started reading.

Fluffy sat up.
He looked in the mirror.
He saw so many guinea pigs!
Fluffy climbed out of his box.
Follow me, pigs! said Fluffy the Explorer.
We will go where no pigs have gone before!

Fluffy saw a mountain.

He started climbing.

He went up and up.

But the mountain started shaking.

Earthquake! cried Fluffy the Explorer.

Hold on, pigs!

The earthquake tossed Fluffy
into the dark.
We must get out of this cave!
said Fluffy the Explorer.
Follow me, pigs!
Fluffy jumped out of the cave.

Just in time, too.

The ice is slick, said Fluffy the Explorer.

Watch out, pigs!

Fluffy led the way over the ice.

What's this? thought Fluffy the Explorer.

It was a big silver thing.

Inside was a monster!

The monster started to roar!

Jump, pigs! cried Fluffy the Explorer.

Fluffy jumped down.

But the monster was after him!

Run, pigs! cried Fluffy the Explorer.

Run for your lives!

Fluffy ran under a big rock.

Emma showed her dad her short hair.
Then she picked up the shoe box.
"Dad!" she cried. "Fluffy's gone!"
"What?" said her dad.
Emma dropped the shoe box.
"Fluffy!" she called. "Where are you?"
"Here, Fluffy," called Emma's dad.

Fluffy saw that the monster was far away.

He saw the shoe box on the floor.

Follow me, pigs! said Fluffy the Explorer.

He ran out from under the rock

and jumped in the box.

We did it! said Fluffy the Explorer.

Good work, pigs!

Emma came back and sat down.
She looked in the box.
"Fluffy!" she cried. "Where have you been?"
It's a long story, thought Fluffy the Explorer.

Fluffy Shows Up

"Good night, Fluffy," said Emma.
"Tomorrow we go back to school."
Fluffy went to sleep.
But in the middle of the night,
a noise woke him up.
Jack and Jill were back.
Not again! thought Fluffy.

Jack opened Fluffy's cage.
Jill got Fluffy out.
But this time Fluffy took off!

Fluffy ran out of Emma's room.
Jack and Jill ran after him.

Fluffy raced down the hallway.
Jack and Jill raced after him.

Fluffy zoomed around a corner.
He heard the cats behind him.
Fluffy saw a bag by the front door.
It was open at the top.
Fluffy ran and jumped into the bag.

He peeked out.
He saw the cats run by.
Heh heh, thought Fluffy.

Then Fluffy found a soft place
inside the bag and fell asleep.

The next morning, Emma cried,
"Fluffy's gone!"
"Not again!" said Emma's dad.
"I have a big meeting this morning,"
said Emma's mom. "I have to catch a plane."
"Go on," said Emma's dad. "Emma and I
will find Fluffy."
Emma's mom kissed Emma good-bye.
"Don't worry," she said. "Fluffy will show up.
He always does." Then she picked up
her briefcase and ran out the door.

Emma's dad drove Emma to school.
"What will I say about Fluffy?"
Emma asked him.
"Say that Fluffy will show up,"
said her dad. "He always does."

At the airport, Emma's mom waited in line. Then she put her purse and her briefcase on the X-ray machine.

She walked through the gate.
“Stop,” a guard told her.
“You can’t bring an animal on the plane.”

“An animal?” said Emma’s mom.
“What do you mean?”
The guard showed Emma’s mom the X ray.
The X ray showed Fluffy.

Emma's mom took Fluffy out of her briefcase.

"What are YOU doing here?" she asked.

Beats me, thought Fluffy.

So, what's for breakfast?

"I'll be back," Emma's mom told the guard.
She ran outside.
She waved down a taxi.
"Driver?" she said. "This is Fluffy."
And she told him what happened.
"Leave Fluffy to me," the driver said.

At school, Emma said, “Ms. Day?
I have something to tell the class.”
“Okay,” said Ms. Day.
Emma walked to the front of the room.
“Uh...,” she said. “This is about Fluffy.”

Fluffy liked riding in the taxi.
Faster, driver! he thought.

“But Fluffy was not in his cage,”
Emma was saying.
“Look!” called Wade. “A taxi!”
All the kids looked out the window
as a taxi pulled up in front of the school.
The taxi driver came into Ms. Day’s room.
“Here’s Fluffy,” he said.
“I hope he is not late for school.”

"Fluffy!" said Emma. "You DID show up!"

I always do, thought Fluffy.